THE THUG
THAT SECURED
Her Heart

A NOVEL BY

MISS JENESEQUA

Royalty Publishing House is now accepting manuscripts from aspiring or experienced urban romance authors!

WHAT MAY PLACE YOU ABOVE THE REST:

Heroes who are the ultimate book bae: strong-willed, maybe a little rough around the edges but willing to risk it all for the woman he loves.

Heroines who are the ultimate match: the girl next door type, not perfect - has her faults but is still a decent person. One who is willing to risk it all for the man she loves.

The rest is up to you! Just be creative, think out of the box, keep it sexy and intriguing!

If you'd like to join the Royal family, send us the first 15K words (60 pages) of your completed manuscript to submissions@royaltypublishinghouse.com

SYNOPSIS

L ove was never on the agenda for Azia Price. She was too focused on building her career, putting it way above love and even herself. Landing an unexpected job at a top marketing firm was a dream come true. And now that a major opportunity for her to become partner pops up, the ambitious beauty is determined to land the new job role. Until everything starts spiraling uncontrollably once her boss's son, a man too good looking to be true, crashes into her world, threatening everything she has worked so hard to build…by snatching her new dream job.

Kalmon Howard is a man who is no stranger to success. Ruling the streets and making endless amounts of cash are just two of the many accomplishments of this sexy, yet ruthless businessman. Never being one to shy away from the sword, Kalmon does anything to protect his family and empire. And those that try to cross him, always wish they hadn't. After his last headache dealing with his ex, love is the last thing on Kalmon's mind. He's more concerned with diving into new business ventures and he sets his sights on the one company he helped build from the ground up. He never had an issue earning respect from anyone…until Azia Price stepped into his life.

Like a bee to honey, Azia is drawn to Kalmon and despite her mind convincing her to stay away from this bold stranger, their hold on each other is too powerful. But while the pair become more acquainted, hidden truths start crawling out from every direction. Neither Kalmon nor Azia could have imagined how connected they would become or realize how connected their lives truly are. But they're surely about to find out and life will never be the same again. Passion and desire fill the pages of this love tale but most of all, deceit. Kalmon secures Azia's heart but will he also be the person who ultimately breaks it?

"Tell me how you want it, yeah
Call me and I'm on my way
Tell me that you need me, yeah
I'll give it to you night and day
I'm talkin' 'bout Monday, Tuesday, Wednesday,
Thursday, Friday, Saturday, Sunday…"

— *ELLA MAI* ♫

CHAPTER 1

P *ow! Pow! Pow!*

"Oooo, good form! Watch that foot work, sweetheart."

Azia began punching the hanging heavy bag in front of her harder.

Pow! Pow! Pow!

"Damn, Zi. You going extra hard today I see."

Azia exhaled deeply as she gazed into the chocolate eyes of her gorgeous mother. She let her hands drop, taking quick breaths as she stepped back away from her mother who had been holding the heavy bag steady for her. Azia's mother had the face of a supermodel despite being over forty. She had barely aged over the years and her golden honey skin had remained wrinkle free and unbroken.

"This presentation got you all stressed out, huh?" Rivera questioned her daughter with concerned eyes.

"It's all she thinks about and all she does," a gentle voice sounded from the corner of Azia's ear, making her turn to look at the pretty woman sitting on a bench in the room's corner. A grin was growing on her face as she watched Azia. "I'm surprised she even decided to come out today."

"They really have been working my Zi way too hard over there," her mother replied with a disapproving look. "Iman, how long has Azia been cooped up in the house for?"

"The whole damn week, ma'am!"

"Ummmm FYI," Azia spoke up as she began taking off her boxing gloves. "I am standing right here, you know."

"Oh, we know," Iman responded. "Even better so you can hear how crazy you've become stressing out over this presentation of yours!"

Once her boxing gloves were off, Azia's eyes drifted to one of her only best friends in the whole wide world, Iman. Azia's other best friend, Nova, was currently busy and couldn't make a trip to the gym. The trio had become close in high school and had been inseparable ever since.

Iman White had rich cocoa skin, heart-shaped lips, long legs, curvy hips and not the biggest breasts or ass, but it didn't matter. Her body was stunning regardless. And one thing that Azia especially loved about her friend was her confidence, which showed from the color of her hair. On Iman's head currently sat ruby red hair that was loosely curled. Iman also owned attractive green eyes that had specks of sepia brown. Her beauty was unmatched.

"You both know hard I've been working on this," Azia reminded them with a serious gaze. "I'm trying to make partner, something that is considered rare by someone like me."

Working at New York's most prestigious marketing company had been a dream come true for Azia. A dream that she could only thank God for. It was not only the top marketing company in the city and state, but its owner was Nolita Howard, one of New York's multi-millionaires. Although Azia had only been working at *Howard Enterprises* for ten months, that still hadn't stopped her from setting her dreams on becoming partner at the company.

For Azia, making partner was everything she wanted and more. She wanted the self-employed title that being partner brought and to be paid according to her hard work. She'd been a powerful force from the minute she had been hired. Bringing on her experience from her master's in marketing meant that Azia was at the top of her game and stood out like a goldfish in a tank.

She brought in fresh, inventive ideas to the company. Ideas that Nolita loved. The ideas worked every single time and brought in vast amounts of profits for their clients, which in turn brought vast amounts of profits for *Howard Enterprises*. She was Nolita's golden girl. Well that's what she called her anyway, and that's what everyone in the company called her too. And she was using being Nolita's golden girl to her advantage next Monday as she delivered the presentation that was going to send their newest client, *Luxe Fashions*, a popular women's fashion brand, to a whole different level.

The brand was already doing well, but it's CEO, Louisa Walker, wanted more and she had another competing marketing company offering to send her company in the direction that she wanted. Nolita refused to lose her and made the entire company come up with ideas to keep Louisa happy. No one was coming up with ideas that Nolita liked and even Azia had been experiencing a creative block in coming up with her usual great ideas. Nolita Howard went into full commander mode by telling her top five marketing directors to take the week off and come up with a presentation showcasing their idea to her. The director with the best presentation was automatically made partner and the director with the worst would be fired on the spot. Azia was the only woman that was part of Nolita's top 5, and she didn't want to get fired.

"I can't mess up the one shot I have at being partner," she informed them both as she held onto her boxing gloves. "You know how hard it is for a woman to become partner and being a black woman too? It's ten times harder."

It didn't matter that Nolita Howard was a black woman or *Howard*

Enterprises was a black-owned company. The marketing industry was still a male dominated field. Therefore, Azia still had to work hard, if not 10x harder than her male counterparts. That was just the way patriarchy worked.

"You're not going to mess up. You've got this. The woman I raised is smart, determined and resilient. You've got this, ZiZi."

Azia smiled at her mother. Not only smiling because of her sweet words, but also because of the nickname that she had given her when she was just a toddler. A nickname that she still called her 'til this day, despite her age of twenty-five.

"Thanks, mommy," she responded as she sauntered over to her mother and embraced her. "And thanks for letting me blow off some steam in the ring."

"No problem. You know you're always welcome here," Rivera answered while gently stroking Azia's back. "You both are."

"I haven't boxed in a minute," Iman revealed as she watched the pair hug. "I need to get back in the ring so I'll be ready to box Nolita Howard if she doesn't make you partner."

A light chuckle left Azia's lips and she pulled out of her mother's arms before giving her a goodbye kiss. Her mother, Rivera, had started her own female boxing gym eight months ago with the help of her husband, Johan Price, Azia's father who had invested greatly into the business. Azia was so proud and inspired by her mother and father. They were the epitome of a loving couple. *Black love.* That's what Azia hoped to have one day with someone. But for now, her main and only focus was work. Azia headed to the changing rooms so she could get dressed into her clothes and head home.

"I'll wait for you out here, Zi," Iman told her and Azia turned to nod at her before continuing to head to the changing rooms.

Her mom recommended Azia come after hours to get uninterrupted time at the gym since it usually got busy with women. It was a recommendation that Azia had taken once and never stopped taking. Rivera's gym was a very popular New York spot especially because it was one of the few female only boxing rings in the city. It was based in East Harlem, a fifteen-minute drive away from where Azia lived in Manhattan.

She lived in a high-rise apartment that she could afford because of the good money she earned at *Howard Enterprises*. Her apartment was located in Stuyvesant Town, a neighborhood in the east side of Manhattan.

Azia began unwrapping her hands from the boxing hand wraps that protected her hands from injury while punching. As she unwrapped, her thoughts drifted to the upcoming Monday. Her presentation was on Monday, two days away and a part of her felt excited but another part of her felt anxious. She was anxious because this was about to be the biggest moment of her career, and if she didn't make partner, she knew she would be heartbroken.

Azia sighed deeply as she opened the silver locker that contained her Nike gym bag where her clothes were. All she could do now was hope and pray that the presentation she delivered on Monday was good enough to get her where she needed to be. Because if it wasn't then she wasn't sure what she would do.

Keon took a deep breath, trying to ease his annoyance before turning the golden doorknob and pushing it forward so he could step into his mother's home study. The minute he stepped in, his eyes dropped to the little fluffy animal running towards him.

"What's up, D?" he asked the puppy, crouching down to pick her up. "I see your ugly ass owner finally let you out of your prison today."

"Yo, get your filthy hands off my baby girl."

"Kalmon, be nice to your brother."

"I don't want him touching my baby if he refuses to talk to me."

Keon stared up and locked onto the eyes of the one man who he didn't want to see. His older brother, Kalmon. Keon ignored his brother's warning and kept hold of the fluffy pet, stroking her gently.

"Momma." He greeted his mother while walking over to the seating area where she sat. And once near her, he planted a kiss on her cheek. "You good?"

"I'm fine, honey, but I would be better if my two favorite people in the world weren't ignoring each other. What's going on?"

"You should ask this fool," Keon voiced while taking the empty seat opposite her. The empty seat that was right next to Kalmon. He let Diamond, Kalmon's puppy, go out of his grip and she jumped to his lap before landing back on the floor. "He's the one who fuc— messed up my car." Keon corrected himself mid-sentence, not wanting to curse in front of his mother.

"Mom, did you hear something? Must have been the wind cause I damn sure didn't just hear someone call me a fool."

"Kally, relax. Key, stop being rude and continue," their mother Nolita demanded, giving her sons a hard stare.

"Kalmon not only took my car keys without asking, he got my car in an accident and still ain't apologized. So, I'm ignoring his ass until I hear my apology."

Despite how much Keon loved his older brother, he damn sure knew how to get on his last nerve. Kalmon had taken his brand-new Bugatti Chiron out one day last week without Keon's permission or initial knowledge, until he'd gone into his condo's parking lot an hour later, only to find it missing. Kalmon ended up getting his Bugatti bumped into by a truck, causing scratches on the vehicle's shiny red paint.

"So that's how you feel?" Nolita asked her son with an arched left brow.

"Yeah," Keon muttered, remaining silent for a few seconds before deciding to add. "He's mad disrespectful, stubborn as hell and I'm sick of it."

"Kalmon," Nolita called her oldest son turning her eyes on him. "What do you have to add?"

"Nothing," Kalmon stated while keeping his back slumped against the leather couch. "He's bugging for no reason."

"No reason?" Keon finally looked over at his older brother only to give him a nasty glare. "You took my shit without asking and fucked it up!"

"And?" Kalmon concealed a smirk. "You got it back fixed, didn't you? It was an accident so my nigga you need to chill out. And you know damn well that your shit is also my shit. I don't need to ask for your shit 'cause as the oldest, it's my God-given right to take your stuff."

"Your God-given right, huh?"

"Facts, nigga," Kalmon answered, unable to hide his smirk any longer. "So, don't get mad disrespectful about something God gave me."

"Mom, are you hearing the wack ass shit your son is saying?"

"Wack ass what?" Kalmon's face twisted into instant rage. "My nigga, come closer and say that shit again."

"Gladly," Keon responded nonchalantly, keeping his eyes locked on Kalmon. "What you gonna do?"

"Come closer and find out," Kalmon ordered with one arm comfortably resting on the couch's armrest while his left hand sat on his lap. "Like I won't smack the shit outta you."

"I'd love to see you tr—"

"Boys," Nolita interrupted her sons with an unimpressed look. "If I didn't know better, I would think you both are fifteen-year-olds, not above the age of twenty. And what's with all the cursing? Come on guys, you know better."

Both Kalmon and Keon looked over at their mother with a guilty stare.

"My bad, Momma," Keon spoke up with an apologetic look. "He just knows how to get on my damn nerves sometimes."

"That's okay Key, you're brothers. It's okay to have disagreements, but I'm putting an end to this one right now. Kalmon, apologize for taking your brother's car without asking and getting it damaged."

"Hell n—"

"It wasn't a request my love," Nolita warned in a caring tone. "You want me to beat your ass in front of your brother instead? Don't think you too old to get your ass beat 'cause you ain't."

Kalmon silenced immediately at his mother's light threat. She was one of the only two people who could threaten him successfully; the other was his father. And even though he was twenty-nine and Keon four years younger than him, his mother Nolita didn't care about giving them a whooping.

"Apologies for damaging your brand-new whip," Kalmon said to his brother.

Keon read the genuine apologetic expression on his brother's face and grinned before voicing, "It wasn't even about you taking it 'cause like you said, my shit is your shit, but you messed up my baby. How would you feel if I let something happen to Diamond?" Keon asked and instantly seeing the deadly look form on Kalmon's face made him laugh and reiterate, "It was just a question, nigga. Chill out."

"Hurt her and you about to be on the first mothafuckin' flight to heaven, Key."

"Kally," his mother spoke up at his use of profanity.

"Apologies, Ma," he said, giving her a toothy grin.

"At least it's a flight to heaven because we both know your mean ass is going straight to hell, so I don't have to worry about bumping into you."

Kalmon couldn't help but grin wider at his younger brother's words.

"Nigga, shut up," he snapped. "I get your point though. I promise it won't happen again."

"Hear that, Keon? He promises it won't happen again and you know how big your brother is on promises." Keon nodded at his mom. "Okay then, kiss and make up." The brothers both looked strangely at Nolita. "Don't look at me like that. You both know what I mean. Go on," Nolita instructed her sons with a smile while reaching ahead for her glass of cognac that sat on the coffee table ahead.

Keon brought out his fist for Kalmon to dap, which Kalmon ignored for a few seconds before bringing out his fist and dapping him back with a smirk.

"Only good things happen when you two work together. Don't forget that."

Their mother definitely had a point. Kalmon and Keon grinding together and taking over their family business from their father meant that they were leaders of the most lethal drug organization in the state. Their father, Fontaine Howard, had always been a natural born hustler and about his money. When he and Nolita first met over thirty years ago, the both of them had been struggling to keep a roof over their heads. Nolita had lost both her parents at the age of ten and lived with her auntie. Her auntie didn't make a lot of money, which is why Nolita jumped from job to job, trying to make ends meet and keep a roof over their heads. For Fontaine, he'd been an orphan all his life. The streets is what raised him and was all he knew, so he worked his way to the top, bit by bit and took his queen, Nolita, right along with him.

Fontaine had made it a priority to study the streets, instilling fear of who he was to rivals. By the time Fontaine turned twenty-one, he had taken over so much territory with his team, he created a reputation that was to last for centuries to come. The Howard name was enough to put fear into the hearts of those heavily involved in the streets and definitely made everyone know about how messing with Fontaine and his empire was suicide. When Nolita had given birth to their first son, Kalmon, Fontaine was over the moon to finally have an heir. And then four years after, Keon came along and Fontaine automatically knew that his sons would rule the throne he had created together. They were blood brothers and his only two children so he would make it imperative that they had a tight bond and worked together.

As they got older, Fontaine began to teach his sons their legacy while also making sure that they remained in education. He wanted to ensure that they had better opportunities than he ever had and make sure they knew the importance of education. And because of how well educated the boys were, they could use it to benefit their empire.

Once taking the reins from their father after graduating, The Howard Brothers changed shit up completely. The focus with average drug dealers was to sell things covertly to mostly those who didn't even have high incomes. But, Kalmon and Keon definitely didn't focus on selling to crackheads on the streets. Sure, they sold to those folk too, but their main goal had been to take on the rich white folks who had the craziest addictions to the purest crack cocaine on the market. A market that the Howards dominated. Selling to Caucasians was where the real power lied because once you pleased the white man you could fool him and get a nice pat on the back. And because of that nice pat, the boys also had their own tobacco operation, which was not only legal, but easier. They had placed trusted individuals in charge of their drug operation over the years, giving them more opportunity to sit back comfortably and reap the benefits of their hard work. They could treat their family especially, and themselves, knowing that they were making money while they slept. And of course, explore other legal ways of making money because being drug dealers wasn't a forever thing for either of them.

Just under two years ago, Kalmon Howard had opened a casino that today was now the biggest, most popular casino in the entire New York State. It featured slots, table games, a food court and bars. The reason for its success was because of Kalmon's knowledge of how to build a business. He had a bachelor's degree in business and a degree in marketing. Whereas Keon Howard had a bachelor's degree in computer science and a master's in information technology. Just under a year ago he started an app development company that helped start up and existing businesses create apps for their brands. He could also hack into basically whatever his family needed and whenever they needed it; a tactic that came in very handy with potential enemies.

"Yeah, you're right, Mom," Kalmon responded to his mother's comment about good things happening when him and Keon worked together. "Despite how much he acts like he's on his period all the time, I wouldn't want to work with no one else but his ass."

Keon playfully rolled his eyes at his brother before grinning. Nolita was glad to see her sons in much better spirits and talking once again. Now it was time to discuss business. Nolita had been stressing all week about coming up with a new idea that was going to take her client to the next level. Kalmon noticed his mom's stressed out state when visiting her and asked her what was up. When Nolita explained, Kalmon gave her an idea instantly, which she loved. And Nolita's client loved that very same idea too.

"I'm so glad you were able to come up with an idea for Louisa's company, Kal. She loved it and wants to discuss it on Monday. As you know, an unexpected business trip came up for me, but I trust that you've got this under control."

"Absolutely, Momma. Whatever you need me to do, I've got you. Always," he promised her. "Thank you for making me partner."

"No worries, baby. You did come up with the best idea out of my entire team. And I know you're busy with the casino most days, so you don't even need to come in everyday, just bring in good ideas when needed and you'll solely earn the profits from your ideas. Besides, it was because of you helping me make a business plan that I was able to start the company in the first place."

Kalmon nodded with understanding at his mother before questioning her. "So, Monday afternoon I meet with Louisa?"

"Yeah. I won't be there, but Louisa's happy to see you without me," Nolita explained. "Oh, and since you have the winning idea, I expect you to break the news to my directors who will be ready to present their ideas Monday morning."

"You got it, Mama," Kalmon voiced with a devilish grin. "I'll gladly crush their little ideas one by one."

"Not crush, Kally. Just let them down gently and explain your idea."

"I got you," he promised with that devilish grin still stuck on his lips.

CHAPTER 2

T his was the worse day to be running late and running late was exactly what she was about to be if she didn't magically appear at *Howard Enterprises* in the next half an hour.

8:30.

It was a fifteen-minute drive to *Howard Enterprises* in downtown Manhattan. Usually Azia took the train or sometimes walked if the weather was hot, but because of how important today was, she knew it was important she got a cab. Azia's Uber was already downstairs waiting for her. She got in and greeted her driver before pulling out her notes from her bag to read over.

Ding!

The sound of her phone notifying her of a text was heard and Azia pulled it out of her bag only to see a message from her group chat with her girls.

Iman: *Good luck on the presentation, Zizi!*

Nova: *Not that you need it anyways. You've got this!*

Iman: *Exactly!*

Iman: *I've booked us a table at Sylvia's to celebrate you becoming partner.*

Iman: *7:30pm.*

Nova: *Sounds good!*

Azia: *I love you guys so much. Thank you.*

Nova: *Let us know the moment you get the job. Love you too.*

Iman: *The very second, hoe!*

Nova: *Or we fucking you up on sight!*

Iman: *On sight!*

Iman: *Love you more xo*

Fifteen minutes later, her Uber dropped her off at her destination and Azia was walking into the building at 8:50. She was thankful that the traffic hadn't been too bad this morning but not pleased about getting into the building ten minutes before her starting time.

"Good morning, Ms. Price." Carson, the young African American security guard, greeted her.

"Good morning, Carson," she answered, giving him a wave as she scanned her ID with her other hand and entered through the security gates.

"Good luck on the presentation," he informed her with a wink. "I'm sure you'll do great."

She thanked him before heading to the silver elevators straight ahead. The entire ground floor was deserted, making Azia's mind race with apprehension. She knew she wasn't late yet, but she wasn't exactly early either. Workers of the company were already suited up and in their various offices, at their work desks and starting their workday.

Her foot began to tap impatiently as the elevator took her straight to the 5th floor.

When the silver doors parted, Azia spotted a few people walking through the floor and she made a beeline for the main conference room on the other side. There wasn't even time for her to give herself one last prep talk or check how she looked because as she glanced down at her Michael Kors watch, she noticed the time was 8:55am. Azia quickly walked over to the conference room, and took a deep breath before making her way inside.

"Azia!" Her head turned to the direction of the voice and she spotted Sierra, her assistant, in the left-hand corner of the room. "You made it."

"I did," Azia responded, tucking a strand of her hair behind her ear as she strode deeper into the room.

The conference room was where group meetings or presentations were conducted. In the center of the room was a large round table and on the wall was a wide projector screen.

"Nolita hasn't arrived yet," Sierra stated, watching Azia place her bag on the table and remove her suit jacket. Sierra reached for Azia's bag to open it. "But I already had a good excuse ready if you hadn't gotten here by the time she had."

"That's why I can always count on you, Sierra."

"You know I got you, girl," Sierra said with a pleased smile and began bringing out Azia's notes and MacBook from her bag.

Azia placed her jacket behind her chair and took her seat while fresh energy filled her. She was especially glad that she wasn't late, but she knew that Sierra had her back regardless. Sierra was one of the only friends Azia had at this company and she had always been such a big help as her assistant and being a good listening ear.

Azia's eyes darted around the round gray marble table at the people already in their seats. The four other marketing directors were already here, reading over their notes and checking their laptops with their assistants seated next to them. A few existing partners of the company were sitting here too.

With her laptop now in front of her, Azia lifted its screen up and switched it on.

"Golden girl, where's your USB?"

Azia's head whipped around so fast at Sierra's question and her eyes grew large.

"In the bag."

Sierra quickly looked into her bag for the USB again, but she couldn't find it.

"Are you sure you put it in here?" Sierra asked her in a nervous whisper.

"Of course I did," Azia preached, taking the bag out of Sierra's hands and quickly rummaging through it. "I did put it in here."

There was no way that she hadn't packed the most important component of her day. The component that contained her presentation that she was to show Nolita. The more she searched inside the bag, the more time she wasted, because there was no USB in sight.

"Okay. Don't panic." Sierra quietly coached her boss. "Didn't you save a backup on your laptop?"

She had saved a backup, but it wasn't her most updated version. The updated version, the final version in fact, was saved on her USB. And she needed the USB to plug into the room's projector so her presentation would be blown up on the main screen.

Shit.

"Okay, okay. Don't panic. I'll just get my USB," Sierra quickly offered, trying to ease the alarm growing in Azia's eyes. "I'll be right back."

Sierra raced out of the room, leaving Azia with everyone else. Azia's right leg began to shake under the table and her head felt hot. This was the biggest day of her career and she had forgotten to bring the USB she needed. *How could I have been so damn stupid?*

Moments later, Sierra came back rushing into the room with the color drained from her caramel colored face. She went closer to Azia and leaned down to whisper into her ear. "I can't find my USB. I must have left it at home too. I'm so sorry."

"Good morning everyone, I've been informed by Mrs. Howard that only the marketing directors need to be seen this morning. Everyone else is free to go, Thank you." A female voice suddenly announced and Azia looked over at the door to see Nolita's assistant, Shannon.

The director's assistants began to obey and left the room, including existing partners of the company. Watching Sierra leave made Azia's stomach knot and her body was burning up. *Okay, breathe Azia. You've got this. Like you have everything; well most things. Just present without the presentation. No biggie.*

Shannon spoke up again, breaking Azia out of her intimate thoughts.

"Ms. Howard won't be attending today's presentations due to an unexpected business trip."

Oh really? Azia's heart rate started to return to normal. Since Nolita wasn't going to be here this morning, that meant that the presentations would have to be rescheduled 'til she came back. *So, we don't need to present today after all!* Azia's body began to relax as she rested her back against her chair, exhaling lightly.

"But Ms. Howard's son will be overseeing all of your presentations. He should be here any—"

Shit, the presentations are still happening? Azia dropped her head with shame.

Shannon turned her head, looking around aimlessly over her empty back. "Any second now and…Ah! There you are."

The second Azia looked back up was the second her eyes connected with his.

Oh. Wow.

If Azia had to ever imagine heaven on a man, it would be on this man right here. This man who had just stepped into the room like it was nothing. Like he hadn't just made Azia's insides turn to mush without a single word seeping past his pink shapely lips.

"Everyone I'd like you to meet Mr. Kalmon Howard."

Kalmon Howard was a figure that left no head unturned. His 6'5 height helplessly dominated any room he entered. He was very tall and had a body that complimented his height extremely well. His light beige skin looked smooth and clear as ever. Just from the way his blazer coated his upper body, Azia could see the way his sleeves were lovingly filled up. His brown irises were enchanting, pulling Azia further in, even when she told herself that it was time to look away, they told her *no* and to stay until they wanted her to go. The more she watched, the more her mouth got dry. She was thirsty. Thirsty for something much more potent than water.

On his jawline sat a thick, healthy looking beard and his plump, pink lips were outlined with a perfect mustache. His haircut was a low fade with light waves on top. He was dressed in one of the most dangerous combos on a man. A black turtleneck was underneath his gray blazer and matching gray pants cloaked his legs. A gold Cuban link chain hung around his neck with a matching gold watch slapped onto his wrist. A dangerous combo indeed because it was a combo that made Azia's body part that lived in the center of her thighs, fire up with exhilaration.

"Like I said earlier, he'll be overseeing all of your presentations,"

Shannon stated plainly, as she took her seat at the round table while Kalmon remained standing in front of everyone.

"Yo, who's up first?"

Kalmon's deep voice traveled across the room, making everyone shift anxiously in their seats. His thick Bronx accent took Azia by surprise, but she loved the way it hit her ears.

"So, none of y'all want to go first?" Kalmon queried with a smirk as he began unbuttoning his blazer and taking it off his broad shoulders.

Just as Azia had guessed, his muscles were large and the perfect size on his frame. Once he chucked it onto the large table, he spoke up again.

"A'ight, say less."

Kalmon's eyes scanned the round table, looking at everyone carefully, including the golden honey beauty that he hadn't been able to take his eyes off when he had first came in. She looked depressed though, so he wasn't about to put her on the spot. Even though the common phrase was *ladies first*, he wanted to give her the benefit of the doubt since she looked unhappy and she was the only woman presenting out of the seated bunch.

"You."

Everyone watched as Kalmon pointed over at the man seated next to Azia. It was James.

"You're up first," Kalmon ordered and James immediately got up to plug his presentation into the projector.

Kalmon remained standing with his arms crossed against his chest and waited patiently for the first presentation to start. His eyes wandered momentarily to the beauty across the room and their eyes met once again only for her to quickly look away.

Damn.

This golden honey beauty was a problem indeed. Kalmon didn't even know his mother had hired her. To be honest, he didn't know much about who worked for his mother's company. All he knew was that the company was successful and brought in a lot of fucking money. The nameless beauty had an oval-shaped face that housed jewel-like hazel eyes. He couldn't remember the last time he'd seen hazel eyes on a woman, but now that he was seeing them, he never wanted to stop seeing them. She had thick, perfectly arched brows with long eyelashes protecting her deep-set eyes and cute, yet full, juicy glossed lips. Her brown hair was straight and in a middle parting. Her makeup was light with only foundation on her smooth skin, concealer under her eyes and mascara on her lashes.

"So, my idea"—Kalmon broke his gaze away from her to look ahead at the guy he had picked, who now had his presentation up on the projector—"is to have a new logo designed for Louisa's company. The logo will be broadcasted on all major social media influencers' platforms as a sort of mysterious propaganda, the same way Jay Z launched Tidal with his artists changing their profile pictures to blu—"

"What's the point of the logo being broadcasted?" Kalmon interrupted him with a direct question.

"To create awareness of Louisa's com—"

"Howard Enterprises has already used and still uses 'til this day, fashion influencers to create awareness of the company," Kalmon reminded him. "Did you forget about the history of the company you work for?"

James looked over at Kalmon with dread.

"No, no I didn't forget sir, but I wa—"

Kalmon cut him off. "Yo, I'ma take a wild guess and say your name is Earl. You look like an Earl."

"It's James, sir." James quickly corrected Kalmon.

"So, look Earl, your idea isn't original enough and sounds hella expensive. Influencers don't do things for free and they sure as hell won't post a logo on their platform for free. Even if they do post it and we pay them, how exactly is a logo supposed to drive Louisa's sales through the roof? Sounds like a waste of damn money. Who's next?"

Azia couldn't believe how quickly Kalmon had shut down James. He had completely ripped his idea to shreds, which was shocking because after Azia, James came up with some of the best ideas for the company.

This man is rude as hell.

"I said who's next?"

No one spoke up and it was starting to piss Kalmon off at how timid everyone was being. He didn't have time for this shit.

"You."

Azia froze when she noticed that he was now pointing at her.

"Me?" she asked in a low tone.

"Nah not you. The imaginary person standing behind you," he retorted before continuing. "Of course I'm pointing at you. You're up."

Azia sighed deeply at his brash tone but decided to ignore it. Instead, she turned her head towards Shannon, more focused on talking to her boss's assistant than her boss's arrogant son.

"Shannon, unfortunately I've left my USB so I won't be able to put my presentation up on the screen but I—"

"So, you're not even prepared for today? How very unprofessional." Kalmon cut her off with ease.

"Well if you would have let me finish you would have heard me say that I can still present without my presentation, as I know my stuff very well," Azia fired back, glaring at him with discontent.

Oh, so baby girl's got a mouth on her. Kalmon thought to himself as he kept silent. *Interesting.*

"Go ahead, Azia," Shannon encouraged her with a small smile.

"Thank you," Azia replied before picking up her notes and getting up from her seat. She ignored looking in Kalmon's direction and kept her attention on Shannon and everyone else sitting at the table as she began to present.

"I've come up with the idea of us creating a Luxe Fashions jam night where we have only the hottest female artists perform, all wearing Louisa's designs. We sell tickets to fans and give the first 30 women who show up to the venue in Luxe Fashions entry into an exclusive VIP area that won't be available for purchase online, creating more excitement amongst interested women. We also have a competition of who can come up with the best outfit using Luxe Fashions only and hand out tickets to the top ten outfits posted on Instagram. We use the performing artists' social media to promote the festival and use bill-boards including Times Square. My presentation has more visuals, but Shannon, I'm more than happy to show it to you and Nolita once I have my USB."

"That won't be necessary," Kalmon interjected, his eyes boring into Azia.

He hated the fact that she had been presenting to everyone else in the room but him. She hadn't made eye contact with him once during her presentation. It showed how little she thought of him and he didn't like it one bit. But he was surely about to burst her bubble.

"I wasn't talking to you," she fired back, giving him a frosty look.

"Well I'm talkin' to you," he snapped, making fury flash through Azia. "Cute lil idea you have there, but it ain't better than mine. As a matter of fact, none of your ideas are better than mine," he said as his eyes scanned the room.

Azia could only stare at him with more coldness. *This arrogant, conde-scending little piece of sh—*

"Because none of you have come up with sustainable ideas to drive Louisa's profits for the company through the roof, but I have."

Kalmon then went on to explain his idea. *Luxe Fashions* was to host a *Luxe Fashions* ball, similar to Rihanna's *Diamond Ball* event, only this wasn't anything to do with charity. This was to do with female empow-erment and female unity. The ball would be hosted by Louisa herself, who would invite five of her female celebrity friends to give talks to their guests. She was friends with famous women such as Rihanna, Gabrielle Union, Tyra Banks, Nicki Minaj and many more, so the event would definitely draw in interest from fans. The ball would be a female only event and to get in, you had to be wearing a newly bought *Luxe Fashion* dress or jumpsuit that would be mailed to you with your invitation. A few female artists would perform at the ball too, but instead of it being a concert that women had to directly pay for, they would be buying clothes from *Luxe Fashions* to get their invitation.

Azia couldn't deny that it was a smart idea because the average price of a *Luxe Fashion* dress retailed at $116. It was a very high-quality brand and that's why women were willing to spend their hard earned money on it. Buying a dress rather than buying a concert ticket that wouldn't cost more than one hundred dollars, was a much smarter idea. His idea would bring in more revenue for the company and more expo-sure to the brand. It was genius.

"So, because none of y'all have good enough ideas, I win," he concluded with a smirk plastered on his lips. "I guess this would be a good time to let you all know that I'm partner now."

Azia felt her heart drop at his statement. She tried to keep her face neutral, but her disappointment could not be hidden. Everyone could see it, including Kalmon.

"Is there a problem, Azia?" Kalmon asked, uncrossing his arms and letting them hang.

Azia couldn't believe it. Something she had been dreaming of, for what felt like forever, had been stolen from her. It had been handed right over to her boss's son. When Kalmon failed to receive an answer from Azia but noticed the rage growing in her hazel eyes, he decided to question her further.

"I asked you a question, Azia," he reminded her.

Azia hated how good her name sounded rolling off his tongue.

"Well you'll be expecting an answer for a long time 'cause I don't answer to you. I answer to your mother who isn't here right now."

The tension in the room between the pair was growing thicker by the second and everyone could feel it.

"Oh, now see that's where you're wrong, Azia. I'm a partner of this company now so in fact you do answer to me."

"You're a partner to this company but you're not a partner to me," she reminded him with a frown.

"Who even said I want to be your partner? With that rude ass mouth of yours, I wouldn't want you as a partner, Ma."

"I'm not your Ma." She gave him a dirty look. "Don't call me that."

Kalmon concealed a smile, actually starting to enjoy the fact that he was getting under her skin.

"I can see that you and that mouth of yours is going to be a big problem, Ma. Fuckin' hell."

"And I really wish you wouldn't use that word while we're at work."

"Well what do you want me to say instead? Fuckin' hallelujah?"

This nigga really didn't just... Azia exhaled deeply, trying to keep calm, but the annoyance on her face refused to die.

Shannon decided to intervene by changing the subject of the conversation.

"Okay! Well guys, now that you all know about Ms. Howard's son being partner, she also wants to make it clear that he didn't make partner just because he's her son," Shannon explained before she looked down at an email on her iPad. "He came up with a great idea that Louisa loved, and he actually has a master's in marketing. That's why he's here today. Because he earned it," Shannon announced, looking up from her iPad screen to the seated employees. "No one's getting fired today, but understand that this isn't a chance for any of you to slack off. Ms. Howard still expects you all to be working hard on your existing projects."

Azia looked away from Shannon, staring ahead at her MacBook that was open on her screensaver. A picture of her and her parents. All she'd ever wanted was to become partner so she could make them both proud as their only child, and now she had been robbed of that opportunity. Her boss's arrogant son had snatched her dream job from right under her.

Thud!

Azia's head snapped in the direction of the sudden sound. Just behind her laptop was a wireless lamp that had originally been posted by the projector. Azia had seen it when she first sat down at the table.

What the hell?

Her eyes raised to Shannon and everyone else at the table, only for her to see their confused looks as they glanced over at Kalmon, who was now standing over by the projector. Azia wanted to believe that her mind was playing tricks on her and what she was thinking right now couldn't be true.

"Did you just throw a lamp across the table at me?" she asked him, her eyes widening the more she looked over at him.

"I sure did, sweetheart," he confirmed before adding. "I threw that lamp at you Azia because I'ma need you to use it to lighten the fuck up. You over here lookin' like you 'bout to start world war three or some shit, when you ain't 'bout to do shit. So, lighten the fuck up. I don't usually throw lamps at people, but clearly your terrible attitude has caused me to act out today."

"My terrible attitude?" Azia scoffed at him. "You're the one with the terrible attitude."

Ignoring her insult, he continued, "My apologies that your terrible attitude has caused me to act out of character. You should definitely work on that shit."

He then addressed the room, "It was cool chopping it up with you guys for a bit, but I've got somewhere I need to be."

And after speaking, Kalmon picked up his blazer from the desk, gave Azia one last gaze then sauntered over to the exit and walked straight out of the door; leaving Azia confused and annoyed, but strangely turned on, all at the same damn time.

CHAPTER 3

"He did what?"

"He threw a lamp at me and told me to use it to lighten the fuck up."

Iman gave Azia a wide-eyed stare with her food lingering in front of her open mouth.

"He did what?" Iman repeated again in disbelief, lowkey wanting to laugh, but not wanting to upset her best friend.

"Iman, I said it already," Azia said in a low tone. "Please don't make me say it again. It's embarrassing enough that he and I were clashing in front of his mother's assistant and my co-workers."

The besties were currently at Sylvia's, one of the best soul food spots in New York. The girls had been craving soul food for the longest and what was supposed to be their night of celebrating Azia becoming partner, was now a tell all evening of what had gone down with Kalmon Howard. Nova couldn't make it to their group dinner so it was only Iman she could fill in with the details of today.

"But oh my, I can't believe it. A whole lamp? The nigga is crazier than

I thought. I mean, my sister's the one with the baby with his brother, and Keon seems...sane, but Kalmon? Nah, he's on a whole different level. Crazy!"

"The craziest," Azia replied with an eye roll before taking a bite of her mac and cheese.

Azia was under the assumption that she was unaware of Iman's older sister having a child with Kalmon's younger brother, Keon. But she wasn't because Iman had told her months ago about Nolita Howard being the grandmother of Iman's nephew. Azia had just totally forgotten about the connection, but now that Iman had reminded her, the connection had come back to her.

"Wow, this is crazy. I can't believe he's now partner though."

"He earned it as his mother carefully explained," Azia voiced with a fake smile before continuing to eat her food.

Remembering their interaction a few hours ago only angered Azia once again. He was a crazy, arrogant guy, and Azia wanted no parts of his crazy. He may have been sexy, but his attitude stank. He swore way too much and was clearly overly confident. *I don't care how sexy he is, I won't let him boss me around.*

"We definitely need to go to the gym this week to blow off some steam about this whole situation," Iman told her bestie, knowing how frustrated she was feeling at not making partner.

"Without a doubt," Azia responded.

She would rather use her boxing gloves punching up Kalmon Howard, but a heavy bag would have to suffice for now.

"I'm so sorry you didn't make partner, ZiZi. But it's not the end of the world."

So why does it feel like the end of the world? Azia mused to herself as she kept her phone glued to her ear with one hand while scrolling through her presentation with the other.

Hours had passed since Azia and Iman had been eating at Sylvia's and now Azia was back home. She had gone straight to her room to get ready for bed and to give her mother a call. While on the phone to her mother, she pulled up her MacBook and her USB that she stupidly left on her dresser. Now she was looking at her final presentation, feeling sorry for herself and most of all disappointed at letting her mother down. "Mom, I'm so sorry to have let you and Dad down."

"Let us down?" Her mother, Rivera, asked her in a weird tone. "ZiZi, you could never let us down. Ever."

"But I messed up, Mom. I didn't make partner."

"Just because you didn't make partner doesn't mean you messed up, Zi. You're an intelligent, independent young woman. A woman that we are so proud to have raised. Just because you didn't make partner today doesn't mean that you're not great at what you do. You are amazing, Azia Price. You always have been, and you always will be. Don't give up. You're still going to make partner one day, that I know for sure."

The number one thing that Azia could always count on was her mother lifting her spirits. She would forever be appreciative towards her for being such an important force in her life.

"Enough about me. How was work today, Mom?"

Azia spoke to her mother on the phone for a few more minutes and then their call came to its close.

"I'll see you tomorrow at the gym, ZiZi. I love you. Keep your head up and stop blaming yourself."

"I love you more, Mom and I'll try my best not to," Azia concluded before ending the call, putting away her iPhone, and trying her hardest to push thoughts of her failing to make partner out of her head. But most of all, pushing thoughts of Kalmon Howard out of her head.

CHAPTER 4

"Uncle Kal, I can't find my skittles."

"No worries, nephew. We gon' find them together."

Kalmon was currently helping his three-year-old nephew, Athan, look for his bag of skittles that Kalmon had ate an hour ago. They'd been sitting on the dining table and Kalmon was feeling for a snack. Now of course he wasn't about to break his nephew's heart by revealing to him that he'd eaten them all. So, he just pretended to act oblivious and look around the house for the sweets alongside him. But now that fifteen minutes of searching had passed and Athan was still not giving up, Kalmon knew he needed to put this fake search to an end.

"Athan, I'll just buy you another packet. Matter of fact, I'ma buy you packets to last you for the whole month. How does that sound?"

"Perfect! Thanks Unc!" he exclaimed, running out the living room and heading to his playroom.

Kalmon took a seat on the gray armchair positioned directly in front of the fireplace and put his feet up on the leg rest. He had been chilling with his nephew for the past few hours and now that Athan had gone off to his playroom without requesting Kalmon to follow him along, he knew that meant Athan wanted some personal time alone. And he would gladly give it to his nephew so he could focus on his personal thoughts and the one woman running through his mind. It had been two days since he'd seen her and still, she refused to disappear from his head.

Azia Price.

It hadn't been hard to find out her surname because *Howard Enterprises* had a database containing all their employees and their contact details; both past and current. And now as partner, Kalmon had unlimited access to that database. He hadn't been able to stop thinking about her and that smart mouth of hers. As annoying as she was, he was intrigued by her. *Very intrigued.* She didn't seem to know who he was either and that was only an extra added attraction. Kalmon continued to think about Azia until his brother stepped into the living room, holding Diamond close to his face.

"Yo, I see you're getting too attached to my dog, nigga," Kalmon announced with a frown. "Hand her over."

"She's a lil, cutie unlike her owner," Keon cooed, chuckling as Diamond began licking his face. "I might just have to steal her off you. Athan loves her too."

"You ain't stealing my baby," Kalmon fumed, lifting his back off the chair. "Hand her over."

Keon let Diamond lick his face one last time before walking over to where Kalmon sat and passed her over to him.

"You good, baby girl? Did the mean lil man scare you? Huh? It's okay baby, you're back with Daddy again." Kalmon spoke to Diamond as he held her up so that their eyes connected before kissing her small head.

Diamond Howard was Kalmon's puppy that he had gotten just over two months ago. She was a teacup yorkie poo with a black coat and gold markings on her silky coat. He always wanted a puppy but never had time to get one 'cause he was either traveling or just plain busy with his businesses. But the last few months had proven to be less busy than usual, so Kalmon set out on his goal of getting his own puppy.

As Kalmon kept on stroking Diamond while she sat on his lap, Keon took a seat on the sofa near Kalmon's armchair. The boys were currently at their family townhouse, an eight-bedroom house with seven bathrooms. It was the twenty-five-million-dollar house located on Fifth Avenue, upper east side of Manhattan, that Nolita and Fontaine Howard owned with their employees who worked within the home. Kalmon and Keon each had rooms that they stayed in whenever they felt like spending the night, including Keon's son Athan, who had his own room and a playroom. Noticing the frustrated look on his younger brother's face made Kalmon speak up.

"Key? What's with the long face? You good?"

Keon sighed deeply before responding. "Take a wild guess, nigga."

"What did your dumb ass do to Athena now?" Kalmon queried with a hearty chuckle, already knowing his baby brother was to blame for the domestics going on with Athena.

Athena White was Keon's baby mama and girlfriend of three years. She was someone who Keon hadn't originally had his eye on, but when he saw how loyal and down she was for him, he cuffed her. Their only current problem was their argument about Athena's current career. Athena White was a very pretty woman and because of her looks, she had managed to rack up half a million Instagram followers. She was basically an Instagram model and received free clothing, make up and various other free items from brands. Keon initially didn't have a problem with his girl's success and fame. But what he did have a problem with now, was the overload of comments and direct messages that she got from male strangers.

"All I said was she needs to start blocking niggas that go overboard with posting comments under her posts before I start finding out niggas addresses and kill them. And she got offended," Keon explained with a light shrug.

"What made you tell her to block them though? Is she entertaining these niggas?"

"Nah, she ain't. She proved that shit to me by giving me access to her account. I ain't even ask for it, but she still felt like she needed to prove it to me so I let her. She's not entertaining them, but I don't feel comfortable seeing that shit man. All those bums lusting after my girl and shit. Nah, fuck that."

"That sounds like a personal problem that you're having with yourself, Key." Kalmon stated. "She's not entertaining anyone but the guy that she is with, which is you, so you really need to relax. It's not like she's cheating on you, is she?"

"She knows she's a dead woman if she does that shit."

"Exactly. So just stop wildin' over nothing. Your woman ain't ugly so niggas are bound to lust over her. But as long as she knows not to play with her life by cheating on you, then you have nothing to worry about, Key."

Keon nodded with understanding at his brother. Seeking advice from his older brother was something he always willingly did because Kalmon always gave great advice.

"I hear you, Bro. Guess I just need to relax and apologize to my baby."

"You do that," Kalmon voiced simply before focusing his attention back on Diamond, who was now falling asleep in the comfort of Kalmon's lap.

"Uh-uh, don't even think about it, D. Wake your ass up. Right now."

Kalmon lifted her up and held her up to his face. Her cute sleepy eyes slowly opened to look at him.

"Last time you fell asleep on my lap, someone had a lil accident. Nope.

You ain't sleeping on me. No. I said no the first time and don't make that baby face either. Nah, don't look at me like that, D. Stop it. Stop tryna get me to change my mind with these cute ass eyes of yours. Why you gotta be so cute for, huh? Why you gotta make Daddy feel bad for not letting you have your way, huh?"

Keon immediately chuckled at Kalmon's interaction with his puppy.

"My nigga, we need to start thinking about getting you a real baby."

"As much as I want a lil kid, I'm good with my baby right here," Kalmon preached as he placed Diamond back on his lap and massaged her soft back. "Ain't that right, D? You're Daddy's baby," he cooed as he kept massaging her to sleep.

"You know what? I bet the girl that meets Diamond will be the girl you make a baby with."

"Impossible," Kalmon said, shaking his head. "No girl gets to meet Diamond except her dog sitter and my momma. Do I even let new people meet her?"

"No, but—"

"Exactly," Kalmon cut Keon off. "So ain't no way I'm gon' let some random meet my D. There's only one D that girls get to meet and it ain't my puppy. But when I find the right one, then I'll know it's baby making time."

"A'ight nigga, whatever you say," Keon replied, giving his brother a nod of understanding. "After all that shit with Jahana, I ain't surprised you ain't in a rush to settle down."

Thinking about his ex-girlfriend Jahana made Kalmon's jaw tighten. Jahana had been a real headache. Not only had she given herself the title of being Kalmon's girlfriend without him actually giving it to her, she made it a priority to always cause issues between them because of her insecurities. Insecurities she had because she knew Kalmon was a highly lusted after man in New York. She'd always burst out and accuse him of cheating and neglecting her when that wasn't the case. Kalmon was just busy with work and maintaining the empire his father had created for him and Keon. He put up with her foolery for just under a year because the sex was the bomb and he started to feel a little hopeful that she might have been the one. But once she disrespected his mother one evening at a family dinner six months ago, he ended things with her.

She apologized time and time again, but Kalmon wasn't taking her back. They messed around a few times after their breakup, but Kalmon didn't want her getting the wrong idea and thinking that they were getting back together, because they weren't. The last time they messed around had been last month and Kalmon hadn't hit her up since. He didn't want her getting the wrong idea about them because he knew how she loved overthinking shit. And once Jahana started overthinking that only meant one thing for Kalmon.

Headache.

So, getting back in a relationship and starting a family was the last thing on his mind right now. Sure, he really wanted to be a father one day, but he needed to find the right woman to start a family with. Right now, he was only concerned with his money, his existing family and his puppy, Diamond. But deep down Kalmon knew that his concerns were really four instead of three. The fourth concern being the golden honey beauty at *Howard Enterprises*, with that smart-ass mouth and attitude of hers that he was very much attracted to.

CHAPTER 5

A week had passed since the day of the disaster that Azia had gone through, finding out that Ms. Howard's son had made partner instead of her. Surprisingly, she never ran into Kalmon, mostly due to the fact that he wasn't in 24/7, but his presence definitely carried throughout the building. He was the talk of the company, especially amongst the ladies who all wanted him, but he paid attention to no one. Azia heard the gossip because of her assistant, Sierra, who eagerly fed it to her. It wasn't until Azia eventually told her that she wasn't interested that she stopped bringing him up. But Azia had been well informed of the discussions involving Kalmon.

All the ladies of *Howard Enterprises* not only thought he was handsome, which he was, Azia couldn't deny that fact, but that he was also intelligent for coming up with the winning idea for Louisa's company. These were all obvious facts, but what everyone else couldn't seem to see that Azia saw blatantly, was just how rude Kalmon was.

It was currently 3pm and Azia was sitting by her desk, hard at work. Despite not making the job of partner, Azia wasn't trying to slack in her work. She was called golden girl for a reason and she wanted to maintain the good reputation she had built with Nolita Howard by making sure her existing projects were completed to an even greater standard than usual.

Azia looked up from her MacBook only to see her empty purple water bottle. She picked it up and got up from her desk to head to the break-room located a few short yards away from her office.

The breakroom was empty, which wasn't a surprise, because every-one's lunch had finished thirty minutes ago, and they were now hard at work. Azia sauntered over to the water fountain in the room's right-hand corner and unscrewed her lid to fill up her bottle. Once it was full, she lifted it to her lips and savored the cold, fresh water running down her throat. She continued sipping while turning around, only to suddenly see the talk of the company standing in the doorway.

Azia almost choked on her water as she watched him. His presence had not only startled her, but it made a sudden rush of heat flow to the center of her thighs. He had on a white shirt that fitted his upper body lovingly, black pants that cloaked his long legs and leather lace-ups that graced his feet. His professional aesthetic was attractive indeed. He was leaning against the white door frame with his right shoulder and Azia noticed the way his eyes slowly swept up and down her body. The way he was looking at her, she couldn't help but do the same. There was just something about his physique that she couldn't help but admire. The more she looked, the more her heat further built.

She closed her water bottle and focused on heading back to her office, but at the very same moment she stepped forward, so did he. Figuring that he'd walk straight past her without saying a word, Azia continued to stride straight ahead to the exit until his body blocked her path. She looked up at him with confused eyes but also intrigued ones. The way he towered over her only made her flowing heat even stronger and his aroma filled her nostrils, seducing her completely.

"You can't say hello?"

His question was simple, but the way he had said it sounded too alluring.

"Goodbye," she said, trying to get around him, but he moved in the same direction she had, keeping her blocked from the exit.

"Goodbye? Ain't no damn goodbye needed right now," Kalmon voiced with a hardened expression before softening his face. "You looked like you were really enjoying that water. You gon' let a nigga get a taste?"

"There's a cup and water right over there," she informed him, not understanding why he was asking her for water that he could get himself.

"Ah, but you see, that's not the water I want."

"Well that's too ba—Hey! Give that back."

Without her being able to stop him, Kalmon reached for the bottle she was holding and took it. The second Azia tried to reach back for it, he lifted it up high above her reach. An advantage he had because of his tall figure.

"Give it back," she ordered, her face twisting with irritation.

Kalmon said nothing in return and simply opened her water bottle before pressing it to his full lips and taking a sip. Azia watched with wide eyes and a dropping bottom lip at his action. His Adam's apple bobbing up and down as he drank her water had her strangely aroused, but still within her pulsed anger at him taking her bottle.

"Shit tastes good," he commented once done sipping.

"So, you're used to taking things that don't belong to you?" she piped up, making him frown with dismay.

"What you talkin' abou— Oh, you still mad at me making partner over you?"

Instead of saying anything, she glared at him before trying to get past him. However, once again he blocked her way out using his body.

"Yeah you still mad," he confirmed with a smirk. "For the record, I didn't mean to take your job, the shit just kinda happened. I came up

with the winning idea and boom, Louisa loved it. As for your water?"
He lifted her bottle in the air and shook it lightly. "Now this shit I definitely meant to take. You looked like you were enjoying it and I
wanted to enjoy it too."

"You could've just gotten your own water," she informed him, still in
disbelief that he had drank from her bottle.

"Nah, I'd rather have this one," he insisted. "It looked like it tasted
good, so I wanted it."

Azia sighed deeply, trying to ease her frustration.

"You really are spoiled," Azia spoke up. "You love getting your own
way and love taking things that don't belong to you."

She tried to reach back for her bottle now that his hands were back
down to their normal level but failed when he lifted it away from her
grip once again.

"If I'm spoiled, what are you?"

"A woman trying to get her water back."

"A pretty ass woman who happens to have a smart-ass mouth," he
corrected her. "But I'm lowkey starting to like that shit, Azia."

Now it was her turn to look up at him silently, lowkey feeling gassed at
his compliment. *How the hell did he just manage to compliment me but
also insult me at the same damn time?*

He finally passed her back her bottle and she reached for it only to feel
her heart flutter wildly when her fingers grazed his.

Without saying anything more to her, Kalmon backed away from her
and headed to the exit. When he was gone, she sighed deeply. Sighing
because she didn't like the way her body had reacted to his words and
their skin touching.

Forget about it Zi. That was nothing. You shouldn't be feeling some type of way towards a man as rude as him. He's nothing but trouble. And let's not forget, he's your boss' son. Forget him.

Her mind was telling her to shake off thoughts of her boss' son, but her heart was telling her something completely different. She was attracted to this man whether she liked it or not.

* * *

Nahmir: *I'm free in two hours.*

Nahmir: *How about I come over?*

Azia: *I'm going to get an early sleep.*

Azia: *Got an important meeting in the morning.*

Nahmir: *Tomorrow evening then.*

Azia: *I'll let you know.*

Initially Azia had returned home and told herself that the person she wanted in her bed tonight was Nahmir. So, she hit him up with a "Hey you" text, convincing herself that she wanted him, but that was the biggest lie. There was now officially only one person she wanted in her bed and she hated how much she couldn't stop thinking about him.

The more she tried to push thoughts of Kalmon to the back of her head, the more they made an appearance. And she couldn't remove the image of him drinking her water, his physique towering over her and those mesmerizing eyes of his evading hers. The same bottle that her lips touched, he touched also but she wished his lips were touching something else instead. A few other places on her body.

Trying to push Kalmon out of her head, she texted Nahmir asking him if he was free. She needed a remedy to help her forget about Kalmon but thinking about having sex with Nahmir only made Kalmon dominate her mind further.

Nahmir was her friend with benefits that she met one night while trying to drink the night away with her girls at a club downtown. Azia had only been in one serious, committed relationship which turned out to be a disaster because she was cheated on. Now there was only one relationship she took serious enough; the one she had with work. Nahmir reluctantly agreed to be her friend with benefits. She knew he wanted more, but more was something that she wasn't able to offer him right now. Quite frankly, she wasn't sure she would ever be able to offer more to him.

You know what, Zi? Just get yourself to bed. It's late anyway. Sleep and forget about him.

Azia took her own advice, getting under her covers and going to sleep, but images of one man only consumed her mind.

Seeing him standing in the doorway, the way he confidently strode over to her, those pink juicy lips he wet as he watched her, seeing the way he refused to look away from her, seeing his lips on her bottle as he drank from it, how he had been rude to her but also charming by calling her pretty.

"Ugh!" Azia shrieked, chucking her pillow over her head. *This is torture. How can I want a man I barely even know? A man that I don't even like!*

Azia quickly shook thoughts of Kalmon away and tried to fall into her deep slumber, but to no avail, because the only thing she could still think about was him. This was starting to look like a big problem; a big problem that Azia no longer wanted. There was only one way for her to fix her problem and she knew it too.

One hand went under her covers, reaching the top of her satin shorts before diving inside to touch on her hairless center. Her other hand went under her tank top and landed on her left breast. She shut her eyes as she began to touch herself, thinking about no one else but Kalmon Howard.

~ The Next Morning ~

"What the..." Her eyes gazed over to her iPhone only to see the time was 12:30pm. "Oh God nooooo!"

Azia groaned with dismay as she rushed out of her room, heading to her en-suite bathroom. She had slept through her alarm. This was all *his* fault. After pleasuring herself last night with only him in mind, she fell asleep and began to dream about him. The dream had been so vivid and passionate that it had caused her to oversleep into her next day of work.

Shit! Shit! Shit!

Thirty minutes later, Azia had taken a quick, yet thorough shower and was frantically buttoning up her white shirt. If today was just a normal day then she would have been more than happy to have called off sick. But today was the day that Ms. Howard reviewed all submitted projects from the previous week and Azia's project was at the top of the list. Nolita's reviews were at 11am every Thursday and Azia never skipped a meeting. Not one.

It was at 1:30pm that Azia happened to be rushing into *Howard Enterprises*. She was pissed about being late, but most of all, she was pissed about missing the meeting. She arrived on her office floor and rushed into her office only to sigh with relief at who was sitting on her couch. "Sierra!"

"Good afternoon, golden girl." Sierra greeted her with a wide smile. "I was trying to get through to you this morning, but you never picked up. Is everything okay?"

Azia stepped deeper into her modern themed office space. It had a color scheme of whites, light grays and baby blues.

"I stupidly overslept," Azia explained, getting to her desk and dropping her bag on top.

"Awww, well at least you're okay! You had me worried while I was in the meeting taking notes for you."

"Thank you so much for worrying about me. I appreciate you a lot, Sierra. So tell me, what did I miss in the meeting?"

Sierra got up from her seat and began walking over to Azia's desk.

"Okay, well the review meeting went as scheduled and your marketing idea for The Crayon Case cosmetics..."

When Sierra suddenly paused, Azia gave her a confused face.

"Why'd you pause?"

"Because you're not going to like what I have to say," Sierra admitted with slumped shoulders.

"Tell me please," Azia pushed.

"Your idea was called trash."

"What?" Astonishment grew in Azia's eyes. *Trash? That's a first.* "By Ms. Howard?"

"No. By Kalmon."

Azia felt her blood begin to boil.

"He was the one that led the meeting," Sierra continued. "His mother's not in."

He becomes partner; that I can eventually accept. But now he's leading meetings and judging my ideas like he runs the damn company? Hell no.

"Where is he now?"

"Upstairs," Sierra simply said.

"Put my incoming calls on hold," Azia instructed.

"Yes, ma'am."

Without saying anything else, Azia began walking to the door. Seeing that Azia was trying to leave made Sierra quickly head out the door, not wanting to get in her way. She looked like she was on a war path and Sierra did not want to get caught up in the crossfire. They both left Azia's office and Sierra went back to her designated desk. Whereas Azia went over to the elevator and pressed its call button. Less than a minute later, she was on the sixth floor and without even looking over at Ms. Howard's assistant's desk, she boldly strode across to the oak office doors.

"Excuse me, Ms. Price? Ms. Price, you can't go in ther—"

Ignoring Ms. Howard's assistant, Azia barged into the room without a single care in the world.

"Have you lost your damn mind?"

The door slamming shut made him turn around in his chair to see the one woman that had been running through his mind. Her angry tone caught him by surprise but nonetheless he was glad to see her.

"Key, lemme call you back," Kalmon quickly told his brother before hanging up the phone.

He was sitting behind the large desk with his hands behind his head as he relaxed against his seat. However, now that she was here, his body rose up and he removed his phone slotted between his shoulders and ear.

"Is that how you greet your bos—"

"Oh shut up!" Azia yelled, storming over to his desk with a frown. "You're not my boss. You never will be and the sooner you get that into your head, the better!"

Kalmon stared deeply at her and when she came all the way to the front of the desk, he smiled, deviously.

"Stop thinking that what you say goes, because it doesn't!" She slammed the table. "I don't care who you are the son of. You don't get to review ideas and call other people's hard work trash. If anyone's trash, it's you!"

Azia's chest heaved up and down and she took a slight step back away from the desk to try to control her anger. She took slower breaths and her calmness seemed to be making a comeback until she realized that Kalmon hadn't said another word to her. The devious smile on his lips had vanished and now all that remained was a cold look.

"Why aren't you speaking up?" she asked him, feeling her frustrations mount.

"Cause I'm giving you a moment to rephrase all that shit you just said," he coolly replied.

"Rephrase? Why the hell do I need to rephrase?"

"So I don't have to fuck you up."

Azia shot him a rude, defensive look.

"You storm in here," he began, getting up from his seat. "Interrupt me, yell at me *and* offend me? You must have lost your damn mind but trust me, I'm prepared to help you find it."

"You offended me by calling my idea trash," she fired back, feeling small now that he was standing up from his seat. Even though there was a desk between them, he still towered over her.

"If you feel offended then be offended. What that got to do with me?" he queried with a scowl before adding, "Your idea wasn't trash though."

Thinking that she had misheard him she asked, "H-Huh?"

"You heard me," he stated with a sly smirk. "Your idea wasn't trash. I only said that shit to fuck with you and clearly it's worked."

Azia felt her mind begin to race with bewildered thoughts.

"Wait, what?"

"I knew your assistant was going to report back to you what I said, and

I wanted her to 'cause I knew sooner or later you would want to have a go at me."

Azia remained silent, keeping her eyes sealed on his eyes that seemed to be now laughing at her.

"Fuck you, Kalmon."

"What did you just say?"

"I said fuck you!" she yelled, pointing at him viciously. "Fuck you, Kalmon!"

"I don't know who you think you're talking to with that tone, but it definitely ain't me. Come here right now," he ordered, pointing to the empty space beside him.

Azia's nipples sprang to attention underneath her shirt and her warm folds between her thighs tingled with pleasure. Instead of doing as he asked, she remained stuck in her place.

"Come here."

She didn't move.

"A'ight so you ain't listening to me? Bet."

Seeing that he was now making his way towards her, made alarm bells ring in her head and she began to back away. But he was much faster than her and before she knew it, she felt a hand on her arm and was pulled over to the front of the desk. The back of her thighs now touched the desk's edge.

Azia's heart thumped at how close he was. His body was pressed up against hers, leaving her no room to run. His cologne was intoxicating, making her body fire up for him even more.

Kalmon's eyes slowly drifted down her clothed body, loving the way her shirt fitted over her breasts and the way her black skirt wonderfully hugged her curves.

"If I tell you to come to me, Azia, you come." He spoke in a low tone.

"I'm not yours to order around," Azia fired back, trying to remain strong despite how weak she felt being this close to him.

"You're mine and you know it."

"How am I yours when I don't even want you," she lied. "You're rude as hell."

"You're sexy as fuck but that mouth of yours." He pointed directly at her pink, glossed lips. Explicit thoughts of him putting her mouth on top of something long, hard and thick flew into his head. Something that he owned. "That mouth of yours is outta fuckin' control, and there's only one way to fix it."

Her eyes widened with puzzlement as she continued to stare up at him.

"Fix it? How exactly do you intend to—"

Before she had the opportunity to fully ask him, he effortlessly lifted her up so that she was now sitting on top of the desk. He centered his body in between her thighs and his soft lips were now branded to hers.

It was a kiss that she hadn't been ready for, but now that his soft flesh was moving seductively with hers, Azia got ready quickly. Her eyes shut, getting lost in the moment that he had started. Her libido only shot through the roof and her entire body ached for his touch. When she felt his hand move to the back of her neck, inching her even closer to him and his tongue parted her lips, every negative emotion she'd previously felt, melted away.

Heaven.

Just how she imagined heaven looking on a man once first laying eyes on him, was the exact same way she felt about his kissing. It was pure heaven, pure nirvana as his tongue dominated her mouth, allowing her to get the perfect taste of him. He kissed her exactly like she'd pictured him to and more. Like a man on a mission to make her climax from his tongue alone. When his lips slowly pulled apart from hers, Azia's eyes remained shut and she finally let out a breath. She felt lost in her own world, dreamy and as light as a feather. Her eyes eventually opened and now she was looking directly up into those sexy eyes of his. She felt so little in comparison to his towering figure, something she knew she wasn't going to get tired of feeling. His hard stare on her refused to break and she felt butterflies fly rapidly in her stomach.

"Tell me you don't want this."

Azia watched as he reached for her idle right hand and placed it directly over the middle of his black pants. Allowing her to feel exactly what he had hiding underneath. Allowing her to feel exactly what *this* was. Her mouth began to dry up as the heat from his bulge, heated up her hand.

Kalmon kept an emotionless face as he crouched his head down and leaned his mouth to the side so he could whisper in her ear. He let go of her hand but Azia's hand was still stuck in place, all on its own.

"You don't want this dick, Azia?" he quizzed her. "You don't want me to bend you over this desk right now and fuck you?"

Azia felt the leakage coming out of her, flowing onto her panties quicker. He suddenly grabbed her throat and pushed it back so that she was forced to look up at him. Her hand dropped from his bulge, but his new action only raised her horny state. "Answer me Azia and tell me what the fuck you want."

"Yes," she whispered with lust cradled within her eyes.

"Yes, what?"

"Yes, I want it."

"Yes, you want what?"

She was slightly shocked at him making her say exactly what she wanted, but nonetheless she did as he desired.

"Yes, I want your dic—"

Knock! Knock!

"Mr. Howard, is everything okay in here?"

Nolita Howard's assistant, Shannon, had taken a trip inside her boss's office. Mostly to be nosy, but to check on her boss's son. After all, her boss's son was basically her boss too and she couldn't have him unhappy because that would potentially mean she would be fired. Seeing Azia Price storm her way into the office without a care in the world had Shannon slightly anxious, and seeing that Ms. Price had yet to make a departure made her curious to know if everything was okay.

Now as she looked ahead, she found it quite odd that Azia was sitting at the edge of the desk with Kalmon a few steps in front of her.

Now that Shannon had walked in, Kalmon quickly turned around to face her and removed his hand from around Azia's throat without Shannon seeing a thing.

"Everything's cool, Shannon," Kalmon informed her with a casual look. "Azia was ju—"

"Was just leaving," Azia quickly interjected as she got up from the desk. "Thanks again for looking at my project."

"I'm not done looking at it, Azia," he remarked. "Matter of fact, I'm just getting started."

Azia looked over at him with a shy gaze but remembered that they weren't in the room alone, so she changed her expression to a relaxed one.

"It's fine. The project doesn't need to be looked at anymore."

"Yes it does," he affirmed with a tense look. "The project and I are not done until I say we are."

Shannon looked at the both of them strangely, as they discussed Azia's project. Their conversation may have seemed strange to her but both

Azia and Kalmon knew very well the deeper meaning behind their conversation.

"I can assure you that the project and you are done," Azia concluded before heading to the door and walking out.

She took a deep breath as she raced towards the elevator, determined to get off this floor as fast as she could. Kalmon Howard had awoken something in her. Something that she didn't want to awaken any further. But as she leaned against the elevator as it took her back down to her office, she knew that her feelings for him were only to get stronger from this point onwards.

CHAPTER 6

"So, when would you like a consultation? Next Wednesday sounds great! Yes, that's fine. What borough? Okay that's..." Nova's words drifted off suddenly when she heard two soft knocks on her oak door. "Just a minute! Yes, that works fine. I guess I'll be seeing you very soon, Mrs. Koyrian. Yes, I'm very excited too. I can't wait to help you design your new home. Talk to you soon. Bye!" Nova ended the call before turning her attention back on the door. "Come in."

Her sentence ended just as the door swung open and into the doorway he stepped. Her body came to attention as her eyes rose to his.

"How you gon' just a minute your man?" he asked in an amused tone. "When you know damn well I ain't no minute man."

Nova let out a light laugh and watched as he took smooth, bold strides into her office. Every step closer to her made her heart beat more rapidly in her chest. When he made it behind her desk, he swirled her chair towards him and reached for her hand, gently pulling her up out of her seat.

Caesar had been a beacon of light in Nova's life. After being convinced that men weren't shit and weren't ever going to be shit, along came a totally different man proving her wrong. A man that loved her for her. And she loved him for even more. He stood at over six feet tall and had a skinny, athletic build, but it suited him nonetheless. His dark skin was flawless and his dreamy chocolate eyes always knew how to make her weak in the knees.

The way his eyes commanded her attention without him yet saying a single word to her, had her on edge. A good edge that was desperate to be pushed further so that she could be closer to him and have his lips on hers. Her wish was finally granted, and he sealed his lips to hers and her lids shut, getting lost in the passion he had ignited within her. His tongue teased its way past her lips, colliding their warm flesh together.

"I missed you," he spoke up after ending their heated kiss, placing his hands to her waist and pulling her closer to him.

"You saw me yesterday, Cee."

"Doesn't change the fact that I missed you," he replied.

Nova couldn't help but smile at his sweet words. Then she moved back towards him to peck his lips before pulling away.

"I also came 'round to tell you about the surprise I have planned for us."

His words made her eyes grow large with curiosity. "What baby?"

"I've booked us a couple's massage this Friday and a private candlelit dinner at Four Seasons where we're spending the weekend together."

Nova's eyes not only widened further but her mouth dropped open.

"Baby! Thank you, thank you, thank you!" she exclaimed, wrapping her arms around his neck. "Four Seasons? That's hella expensive. Cee, you know I don't like you wasting money on me."

He instantly shook his head at her in disagreement. "It's just right for my baby."

The joy building within her could no longer be contained. She squealed with excitement and started repeatedly planting kisses on his face before a sudden realization hit her.

"Wait. This Friday night?"

"Yeah."

"Babe, I can't. I was planning on spending time with the girls. I haven't seen them in forever an—"

"So, you want our weekend away together to go to complete waste?" he questioned her with an arched brow. "A trip I planned for us to spend quality time with one another?"

"No, no, Caesar, that is not what I'm saying," she said, trying to touch his face but he pushed his head back so she was unable to touch him.

"So, what are you saying?"

The defensive tone and the way his expression hardened had Nova feeling dumb for bringing up her old plans. Her old plans that definitely didn't matter now that her man had planned a romantic getaway for the two of them.

"I can see the girls another time," Nova voiced. "I'm excited for our weekend together Cee! Thank you! Thank you! Thank you!" she yelled and carried on kissing his face off, much to his pleasure.

"It's my pleasure beautiful. Anything to make my girl happy," he said, his teeth glinting white as he gazed down at her before pulling her back closer into him so they could kiss once again. "Now, are you going to show me just how much you missed me?"

She gave him a coy look and slowly nodded, dropping her hands from his body to unbutton her jeans.

"Absolutely."

* * *

"I can't believe Nova has cancelled on us again."

"She said Caesar booked a trip for them that's nonrefundable," Azia replied to a dissatisfied Iman.

"Man fuck that nigga! He's eating up all her free time these days and she's just allowing him to. I can't even remember the last time I laid eyes on our *friend*, Azia. Can you?"

Azia kept silent for a few seconds as she slumped back against her seat, thinking deeply of the last time she had laid eyes on her best friend.

"Shit, I actually can't either. It's been a minute."

"Exactly!" Iman exclaimed. "We need to hit her up and have a serious conversation with her about it. How she's neglecting her girls for a nigga she's barely known for more than five minutes."

"Come on now," Azia spoke up with a chuckle. "You know fully well she's been seeing Caesar for more than a month."

"Yeah, but just because she's been seeing him, doesn't mean that she really knows him like that. But you know what? Fuck it. If she wants to neglect us for him then whatever. I'm just going to let her know that when he breaks her heart, she better not come crying to us, 'cause I don't wanna hear it."

"How do you know he's gonna break her heart, Iman?" Azia queried.

"Cause niggas always do. It must be in their DNA or some shit."

"You can't generalize though, he might be different and actually really want to spend his life with Nova."

"He might be, but if he ain't you owe me 50 dollars."

"50 dollars? Bitch, who said we were betting on whether or not he breaks her heart?"

"I did so be prepared to run me all my coins," Iman confirmed, which made Azia laugh.

Days had passed again since Azia laid eyes on Kalmon and instead of thinking about the moment that they shared in his mother's office, she focused on burying herself in work and talking to Iman. Those were the only things that could keep her distracted. Calling Nahmir wasn't an option at all because every time she thought about him, images of Kalmon popped into her head. Thankfully, Kalmon hadn't showed up to the company in a hot minute and his mother was back in her place as CEO, running the company as usual. Azia started to believe that what happened between her and Kalmon had been a one off, never to happen ever again.

That was until Friday afternoon happened. Azia had been typing last minute ideas down on her MacBook before she planned to head out for her lunch break that began in five minutes.

"Azia?"

The sound of her assistant's voice made her look over at her desk's telephone. She pressed the answer button and spoke up.

"What's up?"

"I've got a caller on your main line saying that he needs to talk to you."

"Who?"

"He says he's an associate of Howard Enterprises and needs to speak to you," Sierra explained.

"Okay," Azia agreed as she glanced at her wrist. "Put him through."

The call then switched from Sierra to this mysterious associate.

"Hello?"

"Ms. Price? My name is Terrence Paul, the owner of—"

"The owner of the best seafood joint in the entire state!" Azia exclaimed, which made Terrence chuckle. "I know who you are Mr. Paul. How are you?"

"I'm great thank you and thank you for your kind words."

"They're nothing but facts," Azia confirmed, smiling to herself. "How can I help you today?"

"I'm actually due in for a meeting with Howard Enterprises soon so we can discuss new campaigns for my restaurant, but I have a new menu that I need testing. I was going to ask Nolita, but sadly she's allergic to seafood. But you were specially recommended so I wanted to know if you would be will—"

"When and where do you need me?" Azia quickly agreed, making Terrence laugh even more.

"I'm aware it's your lunch break in a few minutes so right now would be great."

Azia shut her MacBook's screen and leaped up out of her seat before shouting, "I'm on my way!"

"Great. There's a car waiting for you downstairs already."

"Oh really? How thoughtful of you," Azia commented. "I'll see you soon, Mr. Paul."

"See you soon, Ms. Price!"

Azia got her bag and headed downstairs to find the car that Mr. Paul had mentioned was waiting for her with a driver. The drive to Mr. Paul's restaurant was about thirty minutes away from *Howard Enterprises*. It was in the upper east side of Manhattan and when she arrived, she was greeted by Mr. Paul at the front entrance. Mr. Paul was an average height man with ivory, smooth shaven skin and slicked back, sandy blonde hair.

"Ms. Price, so glad you could make it!"

"Thank you so much for personally inviting me," she thanked him, smiling wide as he led her through his packed-out restaurant. He made the best seafood in New York, so it wasn't a surprise to see that his establishment was packed full with people.

"And you don't have to call me Ms. Price. Azia's just fine."

"Okay, well Azia, you'll be dining in a private, less crowded area of the restaurant," Mr. Paul explained as he led the way through the restaurant.

"Okay," Azia willingly agreed, glad to be at one of her favorite restaurants and trying their new food before anyone else.

She didn't mind about eating alone because food was very important to her and she loved it so much. When Mr. Paul brought her over to the excluded area, her heart almost stopped once she laid eyes on the man sitting comfortably by the round table.

Shit.

"And since Mr. Howard recommended you, it was only right that I let him dine with you."

She hated how good he looked dressed so simply in a black sweater and black pants to match. It was a simple fit, yet it looked so regal on him and with his silver chain hanging off his neck, he looked divine. He had gotten a haircut. His fresh, low fade graced his scalp and his beard still looked as healthy and well-groomed as usual. But Azia didn't care how good he looked; she hadn't been prepared to see Kalmon this afternoon. She looked back over at Mr. Paul only to give him a confused look.

"This must be a mistake, I'm no—"

"It ain't a mistake," Kalmon spoke up boldly. "You're dining with me, Azia."

Azia kept silent and kept her gaze on Mr. Paul, who had a never-ending smile on his face. *Why is he so cheerful?* There was nothing to be cheerful about this situation right now, because clearly Kalmon had set her up.

"Mr. Paul, why didn't you tell me I would be dining wit—"

"Cause I told him not to," Kalmon interrupted her with a firm look. "But you're here now and you're staying, so bring your sexy ass over here and sit down."

Azia couldn't believe how things had panned out for her right now. The last person she was expecting to see was Kalmon and having lunch with him definitely wasn't on her agenda either. But it was clear from this entire set up and the serious look on Kalmon's face that she couldn't avoid this.

Reluctantly, Azia walked over to the empty seat right next to Kalmon's. The way the seat was positioned right next to his made her palms sweaty but nonetheless she took her seat and set her bag's shoulder strap on the side of her chair.

"Great! Well now that you're here Ms. Price, I'll get the tasters sent out to you both immediately."

Azia gave Mr. Paul a weak smile and watched as he left the table. She didn't want him to go because the nerves that she had tried to keep at bay were now making an appearance once again.

"I told you that you and I weren't done until I said we are," his deep voice sounded, making a fluttery sensation build in her stomach.

She looked down at the table, avoiding direct eye contact with him. But her avoidance didn't last long because her chin was gently lifted, and her eyes were now locked on his. Instead of saying anything more to her, he eyed her carefully, getting lost in those hazel irises of hers. Those irises that he had greatly missed staring into.

"I missed these," he announced and Azia slipped him a curious glance, wondering what he was going on about until he continued talking. "These pretty ass eyes of yours."

Her whole face lit up at his compliment and instead of waiting for her to speak up, he gave her a lustful look before leaning in towards her. And just like that their lips were meshed together in perfect harmony. A perfect harmony that Azia couldn't deny that she missed even if she tried.

As they kissed, he let go of her chin and moved his hand all the way down to her waist, drawing her nearer to him as their kiss deepened. He knew how to kiss her with so much passion, affection, yet urgency. It was a kiss that ignited a powerful flame within her and made that flame spread throughout her entire body, flickering her desire for him to life. When he broke their kiss, Azia's eyes fluttered open only to see the amused grin on his 'M' shaped lips.

"What's funny?" she asked, watching as he removed his hand from her waist to stroke his beard.

"I'm just thinking about the bullshit you said the day we got interrupted," he expressed with his grin only growing wider, allowing Azia to not only see his pearly whites but the dimples in the corner of his mouth. "Trying to assure me that you and I were done."

"I thought we were," Azia revealed, her eyes focused intently on his attractive face.

"Now why would you think that when you had just told me seconds ago how much you wanted my dic—" Kalmon's words were quickly cut short and his eyes dropped down to look at her index finger that was now pressed to his mouth. Just that simple touch from her made the bulge underneath his pants expand.

"You don't need to repeat it," she told him with a shy look, taking her finger off his lips. "I know what I said."

"Oh, believe me, I won't be the only one repeating it," he promised.

Azia felt her cheeks get hot and before she could even come up with words to respond to him, the waiter brought out their first course of food. Relief coursed through her veins at the fact that Kalmon's attention would now be on something else. The pair began to eat and Azia ordered a cocktail as she needed a beverage. There was silence between them momentarily, but their eyes did more than enough talking as they couldn't stop staring at each other.

"I'm curious though." Kalmon spoke up after taking a few bites and swallows from his food. "Why did you think we were done?"

Azia sipped on her Pina Colada, glad that she had some alcohol in her system. She was hoping it would help ease her nerves. These damn nerves that wouldn't disappear because of the fine ass man sitting right next to her. His cologne was greatly influencing her too. A man smelling this good had to be a sin or something.

"Because."

"Because what?"

"I just figured you and I wouldn't go anywhere," she admitted with a shrug. "I wasn't your biggest fan after learning you became partner."

Kalmon couldn't help but smile as he reached over for his Henny and coke.

"And how could I ever forget that you drank from my bottle without asking?" Azia spoke in an overly cheerful voice, watching him drink his liquor.

"I couldn't get a taste of the thing I really wanted so I settled for the water instead," he stated with a casual glance.

"And what is it you really want?"

"You," he declared before lifting his liquor back to his mouth without taking his eyes off her.

Azia's heart skipped a beat at his words. *Charming indeed.*

"So yeah, that's why I thought we were done," Azia continued, choosing to ignore his charming comment.

"You thought wrong," Kalmon clarified. "Are you still mad at not making partner?"

"No." Kalmon shot her an unconvinced look. "Okay, well maybe a little, but you earned it. I can't lie. Your idea was bomb."

"Appreciate it, baby girl," he thanked her. "Your idea wasn't bad either. It was..." He paused, searching his brain for the right word. "Cute."

"Cute?" Azia shot him the same unconvinced look he'd given her. "Now you know damn well my idea was fire, Kalmon."

"Fire?" He chuckled. "Now that's a stretch."

"It's okay, you don't have to admit the truth when we both know my idea was fire. A whole concert night? Absolutely fire."

"I know you're still upset about not being able to have your cute lil concert night but that's okay," he announced, reaching over for her left hand that was free of any cutlery. "Cause you and I are gonna have our own lil night where you'll get to put on a special performance just for me."

Azia blushed hard before responding, "Is everything about sex with you?"

"Nah, but it's something I do, so I talk about it whenever I feel like talking about it. Shit, it's how I got here, ain't it?"

"Yeah," she agreed with a small nod.

"Exactly, but if it's making you uncomfortable, I'll stop."

She slowly shook her head at him.

"No, it's not that. It's just that you're different I guess."

"Different in a good way or bad?"

"That's what I'm still trying to figure out," she admitted truthfully, gently removing her hand from his grip. But before she could release herself completely, Kalmon grabbed her hand once again, keeping it with his.

"I don't know what lames you've been messing around with before, but I can guarantee that I'm nothing like them," he confidently said. "I'm not a shy guy. Never have been and never will be. When I want something, I go and get that shit."

"I can certainly see that," Azia commented, her eyes scanned their table. "Setting this whole lunch up without me suspecting a thing."

"I really wanted to get you alone so I could have you all to myself, Azia."

"And now that you have me?" she curiously asked.

Kalmon lifted his back off his seat and moved closer towards her, holding their strong gaze. Azia watched as he dug his teeth into his bottom lip and gave her the sexiest look ever. A look that was trying to enchant her to slide off her panties for this man and let him have his way with her right on this table, this very second.

"I intend to get to know you," he whispered to her. "Know what makes you smile, know what makes you passionate, what makes you laugh and know exactly wha—" His hand finally let go of hers and landed on the top of her left thigh. "—Makes you wet."

Sweet Lord Jesus.

His words made her fall into a trance. A trance where she pictured nothing but Kalmon making sweet endless love to her. Love that made her want to be his for the rest of her days on this earth. However, she quickly broke out of her trance.

"Let's stay focused on one thing at a time," she responded shortly after his alluring words, grabbing his hand and gently removing it off her thigh.

Her action made his determination rise but nonetheless he would obey her way. *For now.*

"So, what makes Azia Price smile?"

"My parents," she revealed, beaming instantly at him.

And now that she was smiling at him, Kalmon just came to the realization that this was the first time she had smiled at him.

"Damn, so you've been hiding this pretty ass smile from me?" he queried with a fake hurt look. "I should fuck you up for that."

"It ain't even like that." Azia giggled lightly. "I told you I wasn't your biggest fan after you became partner. It didn't matter how attracted I was to you, I felt robbed."

"And do you still feel robbed?" he asked. "I mean after all, I did take your shot at making your parents proud."

"They're always proud of me," Azia explained, wholeheartedly. "No partner title was going to change that. I just wanted to make them extra proud of their daughter."

"I get that. Making my parents proud is something I love doing too. They're my everything."

"That's real sweet," Azia complimented him, loving the smile on his handsome face at the topic of his parents. He was a family man and Azia smiled wide at that realization.

"After realizing how much making partner meant to you, I told Louisa your idea."

Azia's eyes widened. "You did?"

He nodded in confirmation.

"I did. And she loved it. She wants to implement it a few months after the ball and wants you to be the one to lead the entire thing."

"Wait. Seriously?" Azia's mouth parted as she watched him.

"Yes," he responded. "I felt bad for taking your job when I clocked how much it truly meant to you, so the least I could do was make sure Louisa knew of your cute lil idea."

Azia smirked at his comment before saying, "You really didn't have to do that, Kalmon, but thank you."

"It's nothing, baby girl. Your idea was good and deserved to be known. You're real creative and I like that shit."

Azia found herself smiling wide at him, feeling herself get gassed at his compliment.

More food was brought out to their table and the pair of them kept eating while conversations kept flowing between them. Talking to him was easy. Easier than she'd expected because their first few encounters hadn't gone so well. But she felt comfortable with him. More comfortable than she realized. They talked for hours and hours; about themselves, about life, about God. Whatever came up, they talked about it. It was mostly Kalmon listening to Azia talk because he loved the sound of her voice and he wasn't one to give up too much information about himself right off the bat. But still he found himself revealing personal things to her. Despite how long they were spending talking, Azia hadn't noticed the time and Kalmon hadn't bothered to bring it up. He was enjoying her company way too much to end things.

"You have a puppy?"

"Yeah I do. That's my baby."

"You really have a puppy?" she questioned him with disbelief. A man as big and tall as him she just couldn't picture with a puppy.

"What? You don't believe me?"

"I never said that," she said, holding back a laugh.

"You don't believe a nigga, huh? That's why you're trying to laugh."

"No I—" Azia let out the laugh she had been holding in. "What type of puppy?" More laughter erupted out of her.

"Stop fuckin' laughing, Azia. Ain't shit funny. Why you laughing?"

"Cause I can't picture you with one," she voiced with one last giggle. "Do you have a picture of her?"

"Nah I don't," he lied. "But it's cool cause you don't need a picture. You're seeing her in person."

"I am?"

'You know what? I bet the next girl that meets Diamond will be the girl you make a baby with.' Keon's words echoed in Kalmon's head, but he quickly shook them away. *That's just Key's ass being superstitious. Ain't shit really true.*

"You are," Kalmon confirmed with a determined nod.

"You sure you want me to meet your baby?" Azia asked him with an amused look before her eyes wandered down to her wrist. "Shit, is that the time?" She glanced down at her gold watch with bulging eyes. "I gotta get going."

"Yeah you're right, we do need to get going."

Azia's eyes raised to him with curiosity.

"We?"

"Yes we," he confirmed, his eyes hard on her. "You're not just seeing my puppy but you're staying with me tonight, Azia. Like I told you before we're not done. Nowhere near done. You think now that I have your sexy ass all to myself, I'm letting you go?"

She felt her cheeks grow warm at his rhetorical question.

"Hell no," he continued, boldly. "I've watched you taste your food for the past couple hours but tonight it's your turn to watch me taste you. I'm sliding up inside you for the rest of the night."

She took in the sight of his handsome face with that serious, yet lustful look. She wanted to speak up, but she didn't know what to say. Every inch of her body now craved his touch whether she liked it or not.

"We're leaving now, Azia."

CHAPTER 7

"I thought... mmh... you wanted... hmm... me to meet... your puppy... mmh, Kalmon."

He stopped kissing on her neck and reached for her throat, squeezing on it which immediately made her smile.

"You know damn well I didn't bring you over here to just meet my puppy," Kalmon voiced firmly. "Besides, she's with my brother tonight so you'll meet her tomorrow."

"Oh, so you tricked me?" Azia questioned him with an arched brow. "She was never here in the first place."

Kalmon let out a light chuckle before unwrapping his hand from her throat and moving his hands to the buttons of her shirt. Azia felt her excitement build as she watched him undo her buttons, one by one. While he unbuttoned, she stepped out of her heels.

"I never told you that you were meeting her tonight, I simply said you were meeting her in person," he explained coolly, his eyes focused on her half open shirt. "A day was never mentioned; you assumed that shit all by yourself, Azia."

Azia pouted at him before breaking into a delighted smile seeing the look on his face as he examined her fully open shirt.

Azia only liked rocking lace underwear. It was her favorite material on this entire planet. Today she had decided to wear a red lace set and she was glad that she had. Because the way Kalmon's eyes were widening and the way he was biting his lips was telling her that she had made the right decision indeed.

"You like what you see?" she asked him in a coy tone.

"Fuck yeah," he said in a low tone, his eyes glued on her breasts that were cupped by her lace bra. "I was planning to get you completely naked, but now that I see you have this sexy shit on, you're keeping that on for me."

Azia's smile only got wider and just before she could respond, Kalmon removed her shirt off her body, chucking it to the side before sliding down her skirt, leaving her in nothing but her red lace lingerie.

They hadn't even made it to his bedroom yet. Things had been tense between them from the moment they washed their hands, left the seafood restaurant and entered his Bentley SUV. The pair sat in the backseat while Kalmon's driver drove. Even though she didn't know Kalmon very well, one thing she knew for certain was that he wasn't playing about wanting her. And knowing that, only made her want him even more. During the drive, they both would steal lustful glances at each other without exchanging words. No words needed to be said though. They both knew what this was. They both knew what was going down tonight.

Kalmon lifted both her thighs up and wrapped them around his torso as he led the way upstairs to his bedroom. His lips landed on her neck again, peppering her skin with sweet kisses while her hands stroked the back of his head. *Fuck, she smells so damn good.* Her coconut scent had his manhood hardening with each passing second and her gentle moaning sounds made him want to be inside her now more than ever.

Once inside his bedroom and by his king-sized bed, Kalmon chucked her off his body.

Azia felt her back hit his soft mattress and she looked up to see him towering over the shaking bed. She began to marvel at the sight of him stripping from his clothing. First went his sweater that he slowly slid over his head and dropped to the floor. Then went his black vest, which revealed the fantastic sight hiding underneath. The sight of his abdominal muscles made her breathing get caught in her throat. *Lord have mercy, this man is a problem indeed.* His arm tattoos on his light beige colored skin looked like a perfect work of art, fit only for a king. And tonight, a king he was. The king that ruled over her body in any way that he saw fit. When he pulled down his pants and boxers, Azia swore she was dreaming. She had to be dreaming because that thing between his thighs couldn't have been real. There was no way that was about to enter inside her. *He's even bigger than Nahmir. Damn, can I really take it?*

"Yo Azia, don't even think about it," Kalmon spoke up with seriousness as he walked closer to the edge of the bed.

She gave him a shy look, feeling herself get wetter at the sight of him in all his glory. He could read her apprehension without even hearing her talk yet.

"You can take it," he ordered, pulling her ankle and sliding her down the bed so she was now directly below him.

Azia looked up at him carefully, beginning to get lost in those chestnut pools of his. She felt his fingers slide down the middle of her chest and run between her thighs, all the way down to her panties. The way his fingers swept down her body was the same way his eyes did.

"Would you look at that," he commented as he pressed his fingers against the lace fabric shielding her hairless pussy, sinking his teeth into his bottom lip. "Fuck, you so damn wet baby."

"Uhhh," Azia helplessly whimpered when he began rubbing on her soft opening. He was rubbing on her exact spot that ached with arousal and it was driving her insane.

"Shit, look at how wet you are for me. Why you so wet, Azia?"

His teasing tone only made her mind go cloudy with lust for him. She could not only hear the teasing in his voice, but she could see it in his eyes. And the way he was rubbing faster and faster into her soft folds, Azia felt like she was being teased further.

"Why the hell are you so mothafuckin' wet?"

"Kalmonnnn. Ahhhh."

"I asked you a question, Azia," he reminded her before pushing his fingers over her lace and suddenly thrusting two inside her, making her gasp and arch her back off the bed. "Answer it."

"I-I-"

Her breaths quickened and she felt the pressure between her thighs build as he fingered her tightness. In and out his thick fingers skillfully moved with those sexy eyes of his completely stuck on her.

"Answer me," he demanded, refusing to slow down.

"Becausaaaah Kal... cause... I want... I want you." She managed to make out between her moans and cries.

A cocky grin formed on his lips, revealing his perfect white teeth and he kept on delving his fingers into her until her orgasm blasted right through her.

Azia marveled at the sight of him removing his fingers out of her and lifting them to his lips. Seeing him lick her juices off his skin and groan while doing it, turned her all the way on. This man was truly a sex god.

"You taste real good," he complimented her, watching her catch her breath as he finished sucking her juices off his flesh. "Do you know how good you taste?"

She had just started catching her breath and now he was making her breathless again. Instead of saying anything to him, Azia lifted her hand to reach for his hand, which she brought to her mouth before slowly and sensually sucking his fingers. Kalmon's shaft only lengthened as he watched Azia tasting her nectar off his fingers, and at this point he couldn't take it anymore. He needed to be inside her. *Now.*

Kalmon pulled his fingers out her mouth and wasted no time getting right down to business. He positioned himself right in the center of her thighs and didn't even bother taking off her underwear completely. He simply pulled them to the side before gently easing himself into her.

"Oh my God."

Azia swore she saw stars. Those had to be stars she was seeing even though her eyes were now tightly shut. The intense pleasure that had formed down below had resulted in her closing her eyes. Keeping them open was no longer an option. At first, he started off slow, trying to get her comfortable and well acquainted with his large size. But starting off slow was not going to last for long.

"Kal...mon." She breathlessly moaned his name as his penetrations sank into her core perfectly.

"Open your eyes, Azia," he ordered and she instantly obeyed. "Why you tryna hide from me? Uh-uh, ain't no hiding tonight while I've...ah shit...while I've got you creaming on my dick."

How did a stranger like him know exactly how to make her feel this good? How did he know how to provide her with these mind-blowing strokes? How did he know exactly how to make her body crave him even more than it already did?

"God damn it, your shit is tight as fuck," he commented in a strained tone as he pushed deeper into her.

Azia's hands were moving all along his large arms, unable to keep still as his powerful thrusts inside her only intensified. Her mouth parted wider and wider as each pump filled her and her breathing came out in tiny pants. She suddenly pressed her hands deeper against his muscles as he withdrew from her moist center only to dive right back in, making her dig her nails into his skin. Then her hands moved to his silver chain, grabbing it for support while he eased himself in and out of her. Her action only turned him on even more.

His large hands were glued to the sides of her small waist. Faster and faster he fucked her, loving the sound of her moaning and whimpering for him. If he had known sooner that this was the addictive pearl she was hiding between her thighs, then he knew he would have made sure to have her the day that she burst into his mother's office, instead of holding back for this long.

Unable to help himself, Kalmon branded his lips to hers, muffling her moans as they kissed. Their tongues collided in perfect sync and being able to kiss her while being inside her was only making Kalmon reach closer to his climax. The one place he wasn't trying to reach yet. He slowly pulled their lips apart to try to hold off on the building pressure.

"Ahhh fuck," Kalmon groaned, feeling his dick begin to swell inside her.

He could feel his climax approaching sooner than he wanted it to and he couldn't have that. Quickly, he pulled out of her and removed himself from between her thighs, allowing him to flip her over. Now she lay on her stomach with her back facing him. Her panties that he had pulled to the side earlier, he quickly ripped off her body.

"Kal, those were my fav— Ughhhh, shit."

His thickness entering her from behind had been expected but not this soon. She figured he would give her some time to breathe and prepare herself, but no. He began moving inside her tightness once again and that's when the pleasure built stronger within her.

"I'll buy you new ones," he offered sweetly, enjoying the contraction of her walls around his dick. His hands stayed latched to her waist as he plunged further between her tight folds. "If you promise to be a good girl and cum on this dick."

"I promise. S-Shit Kalmon, it's too-too much, slow down."

Spank!

"Agh!" she whimpered, loudly at the sting of his palm connecting with her round butt.

"You promised to be a good girl."

Azia sighed deeply, feeling Kalmon pause mid-stroke inside her cave.

"I did," she responded in a low tone.

"So why you acting like can't take this dick? You wanted it, remember?"

The fact that he was no longer moving inside her was starting to annoy her slightly. She missed feeling the ecstasy that he was constantly providing her with seconds ago.

Spank!

"Ahhh, Kal!"

"Don't you want it, Azia?"

"Yes I want it," she confirmed.

"What do you want?"

"This dick," she answered, submissively.

"What do you want?" he asked her once again as he slowly started moving in and out of her again, enjoying the view of her ass jiggling back and forth.

"This dick, aghhh!" Azia began to moan passionately once again.

Spank!

"Louder," he commanded, spanking her once again.

"This dick!" She cried out.

"Can't fuckin' hear you," he stated as he pounded harder into her entrance.

"This dick!" she shouted loudly, feeling his balls slapping against her clit as his back shots only got more savage. "I want this dick!"

Azia felt his fingers get tangled up in her hair and before she knew it, her head was lifted slightly higher than before and his chin rested on her right shoulder.

"That's what I mothafuckin' thought," he spoke directly into her ear before lifting his arm around her neck and putting her in a headlock with his elbow. The movement only made the juices flowing between Azia's leg drip out faster. "So shut the fuck up and take your dick, Azia. I told you I was sliding up inside you all night. This dick is the only thing you need to be worried about tonight. It's all yours so be a good girl and take it. Don't make me have to tell you that shit again."

Then he pushed her head down to the mattress and fucked her until she could no longer think straight. Fucked her until the only words she could dare utter for the rest of the night was his name. Azia didn't know what she was going to do because having this man once was not going to be enough for her at all. He was officially the new drug she needed and that scared her more than ever.

CHAPTER 8

Azia's eyes gently fluttered open and she was greeted by the natural lighting coming in through the window that show-cased a breathtaking view of New York City. She was envious that he had such a great view to wake up to every day.

The second she moved her legs, the soreness between her legs reminded her of exactly what had gone down last night and the early hours of this Saturday morning. She didn't mind the soreness too much though because to her, they were like badges of honor, reminding her of the great few hours she'd experienced with an even greater man.

The conversation of them not using a condom had come up after their second round last night, but Azia didn't remember because the moment between them was too enjoyable for her to even care about protection. When Kalmon asked her if she was on birth control, she remembered that they had not used a single condom while having sex. Azia was in fact on birth control, and she monitored her cycle using her period tracker iPhone app, so luckily not using a condom with Kalmon wasn't a huge issue.

Azia got out of bed and headed to the en-suite bathroom on the left side of his bedroom. His house was a mini palace. It was a three-bedroom condo with three and a half bathrooms. Kalmon lived on the top two floors of his condominium building. Cream walls coated the interior of his luxury home and as soon as you entered, you were greeted by his front foyer, then led into his open kitchen and living room. From his wide living room windows, you could see magnificent views of Madison Square Park, the Empire State Building and other famous landmarks of the city. There was also a terrace outside on his first floor whereas he had a balcony on his second. Upstairs on the second floor was his stunning master bedroom, including the guest bedrooms and accompanying bathrooms.

Once she finished peeing and brushing her teeth with a new toothbrush she found in his cabinet, Azia went back into his bedroom before deciding she needed something to cover up with since she was currently naked. She settled for one of his shirts and boxers from his walk-in closet, then headed downstairs to look for Kalmon. She heard him before she saw him.

"Excuse me? Oh, so you must think it's a joke D, but it ain't no damn joke.

"You come back from staying over at Keon's and you've suddenly forgotten how to act. Peeing in the corridor? Now when the fuck did we start doing that crap?

"Uh-uh, don't look at me like that. You know what you did. You know exactly what you did, girl. You're on punishment for the rest of the day. No Pegga pig for you and no treats!

"You forgot who your daddy is, but guess what? I'm gladly going to remind you who the fuck he is. You better act like you have some God damn sense before I knock some sense into you myself.

"Quit looking at me like that 'cause it ain't gonna work. I'm dead ass serious. Matter of fact, turn your ass around, Diamond. Right now. Turn."

Azia got off the last staircase and darted towards the open kitchen with an amused grin on her lips. When her eyes spotted the adorable teacup yorkie with her back facing Kalmon, Azia immediately made her way towards the little animal.

"Awwwww, now would you look at that," Azia cooed sweetly as she gently picked up the fluffy thing. "Aren't you just the cutest thing ever?"

"She's on punishment, Azia." The deep tenor of his voice melted into her ears. His voice was orgasmic. "And you're about to be too if you don't put her down."

Kalmon's eyes raked over her body, loving everything about the way she looked dressed in his clothes. They suited her frame well but he couldn't fight off the temptation of wanting to strip them off her body.

"So you really do have a puppy," Azia commented, ignoring Kalmon's warning. "And she really is the cutest thing ever. Yes, you are. Yes, you are cutie." Azia sweetly talked to the yorkie who was now gently licking her hand.

"Oh, so you ain't listening to me? A'ight, I guess you wanna join Diamond on her punishment day today."

Azia slowly turned around to face him, and her eyes met his before they shifted down to his shirtless torso. Her body heated up at the sight of his half naked body.

"How could you punish a cutie like this?"

"She was being naughty so she deserves the punishment."

"And me?" Azia gave him an innocent look before setting Diamond back down on her little feet.

Kalmon kept silent but his eyes did all the talking as they gazed deeply at Azia. Seeing that sexual look in his irises made her desire for him only heighten, which she didn't understand because they had connected more than enough already under the sheets.

"I could definitely think of a few ways to punish you," he said with a smirk.

Azia slowly began to walk over to him. He stood on the other side of the Calacatta marble countertop. Once she was standing right in front of him, Kalmon gripped her waist and lifted her up to sit on the counter. He leaned closer towards her to give her an affectionate kiss for a few brief seconds before pulling away.

"So you really would punish me?" she asked, raising her arms and wrapping them around his neck.

"Undoubtedly," he confirmed with a firm nod. "Matter of fact, you still deserve to be punished for walking away from a nigga when we were nowhere near done that day at work."

"Shannon had just walked in," Azia reminded him.

"Yeah, but that ain't have shit to do with me and you," he informed her. "It's cool though, we'll leave your punishment on pending for now. You hungry?"

She nodded in response to his question.

"Good, cause brunch is on the way," he explained, caressing her body through his shirt that she wore. "I was gonna cook but I couldn't be bothered. Besides your ass was still knocked out so I just figured it'll be best to order some shit."

"You can cook?" Her eyes grew large with interest but also surprise.

"Yo, respect me. Of course I can cook. What? You think I can't?"

"I never said that, I'm just surprised," she responded with a toothy grin. "Not many guys know how to. Your mom teach you?"

"Yeah she did. I learned from the best, so I promise to surprise you even more once you try my cooking."

Azia's excitement built at his words. She'd never had a man cook for her before so she was definitely looking forward to Kalmon's cooking.

"Can't wait." She concluded before moving forward so that she could press her lips to his soft ones again.

It was only a few short minutes later that catering arrived with their brunch meal. A whole entire cart of food arrived in fact. Azia was gassed to know that Kalmon's condominium came with a fully staffed catering kitchen. So, if Kalmon never wanted to cook again a day in his life, he had that option because there were people who would happily cook all his meals for him. Whenever he felt too tired or just too lazy to cook, catering was his saving grace. And what made it even better was the fact that their food tasted delicious.

Azia eagerly ate her waffles and golden syrup, totally pleased with their taste. Right now, the pair were having their meal on the terrace and Azia couldn't deny how pleased she was. This wasn't exactly how she planned to spend her early Saturday afternoon, but she wasn't complaining at all.

"I like how you look eating those waffles." Kalmon spoke up confidently.

Azia gave him a shy look as she swallowed her food.

"You do?"

"Yeah, you look sexy as fuck," he said, which instantly made her cheeks go hot and she just knew she was turning red. "Makes me wonder what else you'll look good eating."

She reached over for her mimosa, sipping it quickly to ease the dryness now forming in her throat. A dryness that wasn't forming because she was thirsty for an actual drink, but rather for the man sitting right opposite her.

"I'm not gonna lie to you, Azia, I don't want you leaving me so soon today."

"Who said anything about me leaving yet?"

He smiled at her confident words.

"Good, 'cause I want you here with me for as long as I like."

"You sure loving getting your way don't you?" She questioned him, curiously.

"And you sure know how to ask a lotta questions, Zi."

She shot him an amused expression before reaching over the table for a red grape and popping it into her mouth.

"Besides, Diamond wants you here even more than I do it seems."

Diamond was currently on the other side of the terrace door watching Kalmon and Azia eat their brunch outside. Just seeing her cute little face through the glass melted Azia's heart. She really was the cutest dog ever.

"For her, I'd stay here any day, anytime," Azia promised with her eyes fixed on Diamond's.

"Oh, for her only huh?"

Azia's head turned back in his direction.

"Yup," she confirmed in a teasing tone. "For her only, and maybe for someone else who happens to own her."

Kalmon cracked a small smile at her words before reaching over for his champagne flute and lifting his mimosa to his lips. Everything about this woman sitting in front of him he was liking. Her undeniable beauty, her confidence and even that smart-ass mouth of hers was starting to grow on him. Keeping her around for a little while longer was definitely something he planned to do.

CHAPTER 9

"And where have you been, Ms. Price?"

"Somewhere."

Azia's cheeks grew warm and her lips curled into a smile at the memory of her intimate moments with...*him*.

"Oh wow, you know what? You don't even have to tell me where you've been. It's written all over your face. You've been getting your back blown! That's why you decided to pull a Nova on me and cancel our Saturday plans."

Azia bellowed out in laughter at Iman's words and her cheeks only got hotter.

Even though Nova had cancelled on Azia and Iman, they both decided to still go out together to grab some drinks and something to eat. That was before Azia got busy with Kalmon. However, now that today was Sunday evening Azia was finally back home and Iman had popped up at her crib, which wasn't a surprise 'cause they lived in the same apartment complex. Azia lived on the fifth floor whereas Iman lived on the eighth.

"And you're blushing nonstop? Bitch, Nahmir ain't never had you looking like this so I know for a fact this must be some new dick. You got some new dick and didn't tell me? Bitchhhhh, you ain't right! Keeping secrets from your girl? Oh I see how it is."

"Iman, it ain't even like that," Azia admitted with a quiet giggle. "I was going to tell you. It just happened so damn fast."

"Well, you better be prepared to tell me all about it very fast," Iman responded, sitting up on Azia's bed. "Who is it?"

The besties were currently in Azia's bedroom, and Azia was standing by the edge of her bed while Iman lay on it.

"I've told you about him before." Azia climbed on top of her bed and took the empty bed space next to Iman.

"You have?" Iman's eyes filled with wonder. "How long ago did yo— wait a minute... you mean? Wait a minute... Kalmon Howard's been blowing your back out?"

Azia said nothing in response, but the joy cradled in her eyes told Iman the answer to her question.

"You freaky heifer! You're getting your back blown by your boss's son and my nephew's uncle," Iman announced with a grin. "You go, girl!"

Azia laughed at Iman's exclamation.

"So how was it?"

"Out of this world."

"Oh my." Iman clutched her chest. "That good, huh?"

"Iman he put me in a headlock while hitting it from the back."

Iman's mouth dropped wide open.

"Oh my God. A headlock?" Iman's eyes filled with excitement.

"A headlock girl. Shit had me gushing like a fountain."

Azia smiled happily at the flashback of her private moment with Kalmon.

"Oh wowwwww! No wonder chicks be breaking their necks tryna get attention from The Howard brothers. Wait, so how did you guys even end up having sex in the first place?"

Azia then went on to explain how things had started to build between her and Kalmon. From when they had clashed in their first meeting together, him drinking from her water bottle and then the lunch he had planned for the both of them.

"Nah, I'm real happy for you girl. Now you have two niggas on speed dial. Kalmon and Nahmir."

"I'm not planning to mess around with both of them at the same time," Azia revealed with a frown.

"Ummm, why not?" Iman shot her a confused look. "Niggas juggle females in rotation all the time. If I had two fine ass men wanting me the way these two want you, baby I'd be finessing this entire situation."

"I don't have room for a relationship, so what makes you think I have time to juggle around two men?" Azia asked before adding, "Kalmon doesn't seem like the sharing type anyways."

"What makes you say that?"

"Well he's very assertive about what he wa—"

Knock! Knock!

The sound of knocking on her front door made Azia stop talking and turn to look at her bedroom door.

"You expecting someone?" Iman queried.

"No," Azia said as she moved down to the edge of her bed before getting off. "Let me go see who it is."

Getting to her front door and seeing Nova was a very huge surprise.

"Look at the stranger I haven't seen in like forever! Iman! You won't believe who's here right now!"

"Who?" Iman loudly asked from Azia's room.

"Nova!"

"You're lying! She's too busy with her man to be here right now."

Nova playfully rolled her eyes before making her way inside Azia's home.

Standing at 5'7, Nova Harris was a kindhearted soul and that was one of the many long list of reasons why Azia knew that they would always be friends. She put others before herself, which was a noble thing, but also a downside at times; especially when it came to men. With warm caramel skin, captivating brown eyes, loosely curled brown hair that was currently braided into a Fulani style, perfectly arched brows, and small, yet full lips, Nova was a beauty that never failed to capture the attention of her male counterparts. But her heart was smitten by one man only. A man that was taking up all her time these days.

"No way, it must be a ghost," Iman commented as she stepped into Azia's living room and spotted Nova. "Cause the real Nova cancelled on us last minute for some dick."

"Guys, I'm so sorry for cancelling, but Caesar really just wanted us to spend some quality time together."

"You always spend quality time together though," Azia reminded Nova, watching her remove her denim jacket and hang it up on the hanger. "That's why we hardly see you nowadays."

"And we really don't appreciate you neglecting us, Nova," Iman stated with her arms now crossed. "Cause when that nigga breaks your heart, you won't be neglecting us th—"

"What Iman means to say is that we would just like it if you didn't push our friendship to the side," Azia intervened, throwing Iman a side eye. "We care about you Nova and you've never been the type to let a guy dictate how you move."

"But Caesar's not dictating how I move. We've just been spending a lot of time together and I admit, it's put a strain on my free time. But I hear what you guys are saying and I promise that I'll make more time for you both. I'm sorry it's been so long since we've hung out."

"Sorry just doesn't cut it these days though," Iman spoke up. "How about you buy me a new bag?"

Nova let out a giggle at Iman's words while Azia walked up to Nova.

"I don't know why you're laughing hoe; I'm being dead ass serious."

"I've missed you, Va," Azia told her, pulling her in for a hug.

"Missed you more, Zi. Sorry you didn't make partner. What idiot made it instead?" Nova queried as their loving embrace ended.

"Well he ain't no idiot 'cause he's been blowing her back out for the last 24 hours."

"What?" Nova looked over at Azia with a strange look. "I thought you said you weren't feeling any of the guys at work?"

"This one is someone completely new," Iman preached as she headed over to Azia's living room. "See what happens when you ditch us for your man? You miss the whole tea."

"Well I'm here now, so fill me in. Now!"

"Okay, okay," Azia promised, watching the pair of them head to her sofas. "I got you. Let me just grab something for us to drink."

Moments later, Azia had grabbed a bottle of red wine and three glasses which she brought over to her best friends and began pouring out for them. Once they each had their glasses filled, Azia began to fill Nova in on what was happening with Nolita's son, Kalmon Howard. But the dread on Nova's face, five minutes into Azia's story had Azia concerned.

"Nova, what's with the face? Are you okay?"

Nova took a large gulp from her red wine, lifting it high so that its entire contents went into her mouth. Both Iman and Azia couldn't believe how fast she finished her drink.

"Well damn girl, what's up with you?" Iman asked.

"I know Kalmon."

Azia's heart almost stopped at her friend's announcement.

"What do you mean you know him? How? You've fucked him too?" Iman constantly threw questions Nova's way.

Nova shook her head before exhaling deeply then speaking up, "Jahana, my cousin; that's his girlfriend."

He has a girlfriend? Azia mused to herself with a bated breath.

"Wait, what? The nigga has a girlfriend?" Iman's face twisted into fury. "What a hoe!"

Azia's entire body felt like it had gone cold. Like the entire vibrancy running through her flesh had been stolen. It was bad enough that he had a girlfriend, but to now know that her best friend had a direct connection to his girlfriend made everything ten times worse.

"Are you sure they're still together? Because the way he was pursuing Zi sure sounds like he's single."

"I mean, I last spoke to Jahana a few weeks ago and she never mentioned anything about them breaking up," Nova replied.

"I think you should call her," Iman suggested.

"Iman no, it's not that deep at al—"

"Umm, yes it is." Iman cut Azia off. "Nova doesn't even know if they're still together and if they are still together then you deserve to know."

Iman definitely had a point. Azia deserved to know the truth about whether or not Kalmon was in a relationship or not. Her last relationship had ended because of cheating and Azia didn't want to be the cause of someone else's relationship ending because of infidelity caused by her. Especially not someone who happened to be Nova's cousin, because she had a very strong feeling that it would ruin their friendship.

"Alright, I'll call her." Nova agreed, placing her empty wine glass on the opposite coffee table before bringing out her phone.

Azia and Iman both observed as Nova tapped on her bright screen for a few seconds and then placed her phone on loudspeaker. After two rings the call was finally answered.

"Nova?"

Jahana's gentle voice sounded through Azia's apartment.

"Hey Jahana!" Nova greeted her cousin in a friendly tone. "You okay?"

"Yeah I'm good. How are you?"

"I'm good too," Nova replied, eyeing Iman who was now fake yawning at the conversation, so Nova decided to switch things up. "Just happy with my man these days."

"Oh yeah, you finally do have a man after all these years."

Iman covered her mouth to hide her laughter at Jahana's shady comment, which resulted in Azia nudging her.

"Yes I do," Nova said with a roll of her eyes. "I'm just tryna be in love like my big cuz."

"Well, I guess I taught you well."

"How's things with you and your man?"

"Why are you asking?"

The defensive tone in Jahana's voice was unmissable.

"Oh, just curious that's all. It's been a minute since we've spoken so I wasn't sure if you and Kalmon were still together."

"He's still mine so don't worry yourself."

That comment was enough to make Azia lift her remaining red wine to her lips and chug it all down her throat.

"Alrightie. Well I guess I'll speak to you soon cuz. I gotta head out right now."

Azia felt a hand rub her back and she looked over at Iman who had a sorry look on her face. Azia shot her a weak smile before her eyes drifted over to Nova who had ended the call with Jahana.

"Nova, I'm so sorry. I didn't know that was your cousin's man."

"How could you have known? You've never met Jahana," Nova told her. "Neither of you have. You don't need to apologize."

"But I slept with him, Nova."

"Numerous times," Iman added quietly, making Azia throw her a side eye.

"What's done is done. We can't change the past, the only thing we can do now is move on. Yes, Jahana and I are cousins but we ain't that close. I'm not planning to tell her what her man did with you. If she's not smart enough to realize that her man is cheating on her, then that's on her."

"I still feel so bad, Nova. That's your whole cousin."

"You didn't know and it was my fault for not making our dinner at Sylvia's. 'Cause I would have found out that Kalmon made partner and could have told you about him and Jahana then. So, if there is anyone to blame, it's me, Zi. Don't beat yourself up about it."

"I agree with Nova." Iman chimed in. "Don't beat yourself up about something you never knew about. Just kick his ass to the curb and only deal with Nahmir. Block Kalmon's number and ignore him next time you see him at work."

"Well, I can't exactly block his number," Azia voiced with a blank stare.

"Why not?" Nova queried.

"He never gave it to me."

"Wait, huh? What do you mean he never gave it to you?" Iman's eyes widened with each question she asked. "The nigga dicks you down for the weekend and doesn't try to keep in touch with you?"

"Well technically, he doesn't need to keep in touch with her because she works at his mother's company," Nova reminded Iman.

"Yeah, but it's still weird. Guys always ask for numbers. The only time they don't is when they're just tryna fuck and go."

Azia already felt like shit learning that she had slept with her best friend's cousin's man. But to now know that he had basically lied about wanting to get to know her just so he could have sex with her, only made her feel even worse than she already felt. He basically used her, knowing fully well that she didn't like him from the jump after he stole her dream job. *I must have been some sort of challenge to him. Something he had to conquer.*

"I hate him," Azia announced with fury pulsating through her body. "Next time I see his ass, he's gonna regret ever fucking with me."

"That's our girl! Fuck that nigga up on sight!" Iman encouraged.

"Not on sight, Iman. We don't want Zi losing her job."

"I'm not going to lose my job 'cause I'm simply going to give him a piece of my mind," Azia explained before reaching for the almost empty wine bottle and emptying it into her mouth.

Messing with Kalmon Howard was now officially the biggest mistake of her life.

CHAPTER 10

"**B**aby, how many times do I have to say sorry? You can't still be mad at me? Huh? You still mad?" Keon asked as he planted a kiss to the nook of her neck. "You still mad at your nigga? Huh? You want me to convince you to stop being mad? 'Cause I can think...of...many...ways...to convince your fine ass."

"Key, stopppppp," Athena quietly protested, knowing fully well she didn't want him to stop kissing on her.

"You really want me to stop?" he asked, kissing her one last time before looking down at her with a toothy smile.

"No," she said as she looked up at him.

"So you forgive me?"

She nodded in response to his question before saying, "I just don't want my man to end up in jail because he felt the need to kill someone who commented under my pictures."

"Jail?" Keon shot her a contorted expression. "Your nigga's way too smart for that. But I'll definitely show up at the nigga's funeral to make sure he's really gone."

"Keon!"

"Joke," he stated with a light chuckle. "Ain't no killings happening... for now."

"Better not be."

"I love you, Athena."

"And I love you too, Key. You know that."

Keon smiled at her words and wrapped his arms tighter around her.

This woman right here meant everything to him. She had blessed him with a son and blessed him with unwavering loyalty. And for that he would always love her and protect her with his life. Although when they had first met, Keon had eyes for someone else, all he had eyes for today was this beauty standing right in front of him. He hoped one day to marry her and be able to create more kids with her. Athan, their son, was one of their six children and they still had five more to make. Keon couldn't wait for them to spend the rest of their lives together, making babies and being happy.

"I gotta handle some business with Kal real quick, but I'll be back before you know it."

"It's late though, Key. Do you really have to go right now?"

"Yes," he confirmed with a sure nod. "But I promise I'll be back before you know it, baby."

"Okay."

After saying his goodbyes to Athena and giving his sleeping son a kiss goodbye, Keon made his way to the location of the many warehouses that him and Kalmon owned. The warehouses were mainly used to store product, but on nights like these, they served one other purpose.

"Is your cousin really eating skittles right now?"

"Let's not forget that his crazy ass happens to be your brother."

"Yeah, but I'm pretty sure he got dropped on the head as a child before I was born," Keon informed Jahmai with a smirk.

Kalmon said nothing and continued to chew on his hard candy while looking at his cousin and brother with an amused expression. He lifted up his sweet packet and emptied it into his mouth before chucking the empty packet to the floor. Then his attention went to the seated man in front of him, and he pulled off the duct tape plastered onto the man's mouth.

"Ahhhhh!"

The yells coming from the man in front of him did not faze him one bit. Neither did the terrified look in his eyes. Kalmon wanted nothing more than to see him suffer as punishment for what he had done.

"Kalmon, please forgive me! It was a mistake." The man quickly blurted out, which made Kalmon chuckle.

"A mistake?" he asked the man with an arched brow. "Y'all hear that shit?" Kalmon turned around to look at his brother and cousin. "A mistake he says."

Jahmai simply shook his head with his arms crossed against his chest and Keon frowned, but both of them remained silent. They already knew what was going down for Reese. Reese was one of the many men that sold the drugs of The Howard's around the city with his crew. He was someone that The Howard's believed they could trust, until word got back to Jahmai Howard on how Reese was holding back profits and pretending like weight wasn't selling the same. One of his crewmembers snitched on him and here he was now, having to answer to the head bosses in charge.

Jahmai Howard was the cousin of Kalmon and Keon, but also their right-hand man that they placed in charge of distributing their product to their workers. And he was someone Kalmon considered to be his best friend because of how much he could count on him and how much trust Jahmai had shown over the years working with him and Keon.

"A'ight, so Reese," Kalmon addressed Reese once again, looking back over to him with a blank stare. "What do you think should be done about your mistake?"

Reese looked up at Kalmon with an unsure look. He wasn't sure if he really was supposed to answer that question. For all he knew, it could be a trick question designed to make him dig himself into a bigger hole than he already was.

"I-I-"

"I-I- what? What? You can't speak English now?" Kalmon gave him a rude look. "What do you think should be done about your mistake?" Kalmon repeated his question without breaking eye contact from Reese. "Don't make me have to ask you again."

Reese could feel his stomach getting tighter with each passing second and the sweat currently dripping down his forehead wasn't a normal occurrence at all. He was more nervous about having to answer a question that he knew deep down had only one answer. So the only thing he could think to do was lie further.

"Kalmon, I'm sorry, man! Money's just been getting so tight 'cause I need to provide for my mom and I needed to put some money aside so…"

Kalmon watched the words leave Reese's mouth, but at this point, he was no longer paying attention to anything he had to say. The fact that Reese failed to answer his question twice had already frustrated Kalmon, but to now hear Reese lie right to his face was only making him more frustrated. Kalmon had already heard this lie from Jahmai, who Reese first confided in about being strapped for cash because he was helping his mom with her bills.

Reese was known by his crew members to be a big spender. The same way he loved selling drugs across the city, was the same way he loved spending money on prostitutes, jewelry and cars. Money wasn't tight at all because Reese was supporting his mom. It was tight because of his greed and inability to care about anyone else but himself. Reese didn't think that The Howard's knew about his spending habits, but they did. They knew that and so much more.

"And she's my world man, so I just do everything to support her."

"Oh everything to support her, huh?" Kalmon asked him in a fake curious tone. He started walking around Reese's chair.

"Yeah, she's so important to me." Reese continued to lie; his nerves mounting at the fact that Kalmon was now walking around his chair.

"Tell me how important she is to you," Kalmon requested, standing behind Reese while Jahmai and Keon remained standing ahead.

"Umm well, she's my world and I would do anything for her aghhhhhh!"

The sudden entry of a sharp object entering his side made Reese scream out in agony. And he looked down to get a look at the object only to scream again when it cut into his left side.

"Aghhhhhhhh!"

"That's funny," Kalmon commented with a smirk before stabbing Reese's right side again and twisting his knife within Reese's flesh, making him only yell out more. "I spoke to your mom an hour ago and she hasn't received a single phone call from you in months, Reese."

Kalmon brought out the knife and inflicted pain onto Reese once again by stabbing him repeatedly in his torso. By now, Kalmon had moved from standing behind Reese and was standing in front of him, slicing through Reese's clothing to inflict pain to him.

"So how the fuck"—Kalmon kept on plunging his weapon within him —"is she your world?"—the blood dripping through Reese's clothing was endless now—"when you ain't spoken to her or sent her a single fuckin' dime?" Reese could only cry out, unable to speak properly as Kalmon carried out his torture on him. Each stab only caused more suffering and more blood to leak out of his body. And with the amount of blood now leaving his body, Reese could feel himself getting light-headed. Eventually, Kalmon stopped stabbing Reese and looked down at him with an emotionless stare.

"You not only lied to me, Reese, you stole from me. You failed to answer me when I asked you what should be done about your mistake, but I already know exactly what is to be done about your mistake."

"Kal...mon...ple—"

Kalmon thrusted his blade into the side of Reese's neck, stopping him from saying his last few words and observed the endless flow of blood gushing out of him.

"We've got his replacement in position?" Kalmon asked, watching the light leave Reese's eyes and the blood leaving his body. He wiped his blade clean with a tissue he pulled out of his pocket before chucking the tissue to the floor.

"Yup," Jahmai confirmed.

"Good," Kalmon replied with a satisfied grin. He turned around to face his brother and cousin. "Get the cleanup crew in here. It's fuckin' filthy."

"On it," Keon said, whipping out his phone.

"I'ma see y'all later," Kalmon concluded, walking away from his cousin and brother.

Ding!

The sound of his phone going off made Kalmon reach into his pocket while heading to the exit. Seeing her name made him glare at his phone.

Can we talk?

Jahana.

It was only until he was in his car sitting comfortably in his driver's seat that he decided to respond to her text message.

About what? He typed back.

Her response came shooting in: *About us.*

Kalmon: *There is no us.*

Jahana: *I wish there was though.*

Jahana: *I miss you.*

Kalmon: *There's nothing to miss.*

Kalmon: *We're done Jahana.*

Jahana: *We don't have to be.*

Jahana: *If you just took the time to really think about us...*

Jahana: *You'll realize we're meant to be.*

Kalmon: *I don't have time for this shit, your shit or the bullshit today Jahana.*

Kalmon: *You text me again and we about to have a real problem.*

And when her read receipt came in, showing that she had read his text, but not responded straight away like she had been before, Kalmon was grateful that she had gotten the message. Blocking her number was way overdue.

CHAPTER 11

Kalmon hadn't been in Howard Enterprises for a few days now and initially, Azia was irritated because she wanted to see him and give him a piece of her mind. But the more she thought about it, it was actually a good thing that Kalmon wasn't at work because she didn't have to be forced to see his ugly ass face.

Girl, you know damn well his ass is not ugly.

At this point, Azia would prefer it if she never had to see his face again because clearly being in his presence was only going to cause problems for her.

"So guys, let's go over these visual ideas for this new campaign."

Azia was currently in a group meeting with content producers at Howard Enterprises trying to discuss new ideas for their latest campaign of the week.

It was currently 3:30pm and this group meeting was officially the best part of Azia's day. She loved being able to sit down with a team and watch them collectively bring their ideas to life. There was no greater feeling than being able to bring ideas that started off as a mere thought to life, visually. That's what she loved the most about her job; being able to bring her visions to life. There was nothing else she'd rather be doing than this. An hour later, the meeting was finally over and Azia said her goodbyes to the content producers before heading back to her office to look over her notes.

Ding!

As Azia walked to the elevator that was to take her up to her office, she felt her phone vibrate in her palm. She peeked at it to see the incoming text notification from Iman.

Girl, was he in today?

Nope, Azia typed back as she stepped into the elevator.

Iman: *Damn. I was looking forward to you telling me about how you cussed his ass out!*

Azia: *At this point I don't even want to see him.*

Azia: *Fuck his ass.*

Iman: *Fuck him!*

Iman: *Still think you should give him a piece of your mind though.*

Azia: *If I ever see his ass then yeah, why not?*

Azia sent her response just as the elevator opened up on her office floor.

Ding!

Azia walked out and looked down at her phone as she strode over to her office. A new response from Iman had come in but an unexpected sender had also arrived too.

I miss you.

Nahmir.

She couldn't help but smile at his message. They hadn't spoken for over a week now and quite frankly, Azia didn't understand why she hadn't hit him up sooner.

Oh you do? She typed back, deciding to entertain him.

Nahmir: *I can show you much better than I can tell you.*

Azia's smile only got wider as she got to her office's front door and turned her golden knob to walk inside.

Well I can't wait for you to.

The second she started typing her text message to Nahmir, her head popped up only for her to see the man sitting on the other side of her desk. She froze in her stance by the now closed door as she watched him.

Shit.

His comfortable state showed by the way his body rested against her office chair like he had no worries or stress from the world. And to see him dressed in a navy suit had her mind racing with explicit thoughts of seeing that amazing physique hiding underneath his clothing. That physique she had seen naked the night they first...

"What are you doing in my office?"

Her brash tone had caught him completely off guard. And that rude look on her pretty face was not one that he was expecting at all. He had expected to see her happy that they were finally seeing each other after a couple days apart.

"Why the fuck are you looking at me like that, Azia?" he asked her, matching the exact energy that she had decided to give him.

"Because I don't want you here, Kalmon," she replied coolly. She felt her phone vibrate in her hand once again but instead of checking it, she ignored it. "Please leave."

"Leave?" A light chuckle seeped out of his lips. "Now why the hell would I leave when I came to see you?"

Kalmon didn't understand why she was being so defensive and mean towards him, but he was determined to get to the bottom of it.

"You should be seeing your girlfriend," Azia announced with her arms now crossed. The fact that he was amused, made her blood boil. "Not me."

Girlfriend? Kalmon mused to himself, truly confused about her announcement. *What the hell is she on about?*

"And who exactly is my girl that you believe I should be seeing right now instead of you, Azia?"

Azia scoffed at him, in disbelief that he was really playing dumb with her right now.

"You know who your girlfriend is, Kalmon. Don't act dumb."

"The only person acting dumb right now is you who has failed to answer my question."

"Jahana!" she exclaimed, hating the fact that he was currently getting under her skin. He could do it so easily too and she despised him for it. "That's your girlfriend. Remember her?"

This isn't you giving him a piece of your mind Zi. What the hell happened to all that damn energy?

Kalmon shook his head at her with a smirk before speaking up, "Nah, that's my ex."

"That's not what she said," Azia countered.

"So you've met her?" His question was followed with curiosity cradled deep within his brown eyes.

"Something like that," Azia said as she watched him carefully. "She's my best friend's cousin."

"Interesting. And she said what to you exactly?"

Kalmon could feel his irritation heightening at the fact that Jahana had managed to worm herself back into his personal life.

"It's not what she said to me but my best friend," Azia explained. "She said that you're still hers and that right there is confirmation you're still with her."

"Oh, so that's what that means huh?" Kalmon queried with a smirk.

The smirk growing on his pink lips was only pissing Azia off further and she was no longer in the mood to see his face or talk to him. *Fuck giving him a piece of my mind. I want him gone.*

"I think it's time you left my office, don't you?"

"And I think it's time you stopped being scared to walk deeper into your office, don't you?" Kalmon fired back. "Cause I ain't going anywhere until I get what I came for."

"And what exactly did you come for?"

"Come closer and you'll find out," he stated, confidently.

"I'd rather not."

"Don't make me have to come and get you myself, Azia."

His threat made her womanhood jolt with excitement but she chose to ignore it.

"You're not the boss of me, Kalmon."

"But who was the boss of that pussy a few days ago?"

Azia gave him a wide-eyed stare without uttering a word. She didn't even need to speak though because her pussy was doing all the talking as she thought back to the weekend that Kalmon had broken her back in numerous ways and dived inside her nonstop.

"I'm not gonna ask you to come to me again, Azia. You just need to do that shit now, unless you want to get your ass fucked up."

Actually nope! Definitely giving him a piece of mind, she mused as she took bold steps towards him.

"You must be the most arrogant guy I have ever come across," Azia started with a firm expression. "You have a girlfriend and then you have the audacity to pursue me, get me into your bed and waltz up in here like you've done nothing wrong. I never should have messed around with you in the first place when you're my boss' son and now you've played me like a fool. You didn't even take my number once we were done because you wanted one thing only and you got it. I don't want anything to do with your ass any longer and I would really appreciate if you got your ass the fuck outta my office," Azia stated firmly as she pointed to her door without taking her eyes off him. By now she had made it to the front of her desk and was looking down at him as he remained seated in her chair. Even after her speech he still looked so comfy sitting in her seat.

Instead of responding to her, Kalmon brought out his phone from his pocket and began tapping on his bright screen. Azia watched him with confusion then heard the dialing tone of whoever's line he was ringing right now.

What the hell is he doi—

"Baby."

Hearing Jahana's voice made Azia instantly frown, but instead of saying anything, she decided to stay silent and see exactly what this crazy man was up to.

"Who's your baby?" Azia read the disgust on his face as he questioned Jahana. Even though he was clearly disgusted, his handsome features remained intact.

"Kalmon, baby I—"

"You keep calling me your baby like you know that shit is true when we both know it's not. Are we still together, Jahana?" Kalmon's eyes lifted to Azia's, now holding her gaze as he spoke to his ex.

"That doesn't matter because I still love you, Kal."

"Jahana," Kalmon called her name tensely. "Answer my question."

"No, we're not still together, Kalmon, but I wa—"

"Let this be the last mothafuckin' time I have to call your ass and remind you of what's no longer between us. We are not together and won't be getting back together ever again. The sooner you get that shit into your head, the better."

"But Kalmo—"

"If I have to call you again to let you know that I don't belong to you, I guarantee Jahana that shit's going to end badly for you. You gon' come up missing if you keep fucking with me. Do I make myself clear?"

Jahana sighed deeply before responding with a quiet, "Yes."

"What was that?" Kalmon questioned her.

"Yes," she said a little louder.

"Yes what?"

"Yes, Kalmon. You've made yourself clear."

And after her concluding words, Kalmon pressed the end call button and threw his phone down to Azia's desk. Then his eyes wandered up and down Azia's clothed body. Today she was dressed in a tight fitting black skirt and white blouse. Two pieces of clothing that appeared simple, but to Kalmon they were everything on her. Even in work attire, Azia was still so damn stunning to him.

"Just because you've called your ex and confirmed that you two aren't together doesn't make things better between us. I still want you out of my office, Kalmon."

Kalmon rose out of his seat and quickly made his way around her table so that he could be close to her. Seeing that he was heading towards her made her heart skip a beat, but instead of backing up and trying to run away, Azia stayed firm in her stance. Something she believed she would have no trouble doing until Kalmon was directly next to her and pulled her near to him. Smelling his cologne sent her mind into overdrive, but instead of trying to yield into what her body wanted, Azia chose to remain strong.

Before she knew it, he moved her to the edge of her desk, giving her deja vu of the day that he first kissed her in his mother's office. The only difference was, instead of sitting her down on her desk's edge, she was standing while he stood directly in front of her. Those cocoa eyes of his were stuck on her, refusing to break away.

"Kalmo—"

"I came to see you and this is how you treat me."

She continued to look up at him, beginning to get lost in those irises of his. Those eyes that knew how to pull her in every single time.

"This is how you treat me despite the fact that you're the only person running through my mind these days," he told her in a low tone, pressing his hands to the side of her waist.

Azia pulled her head away to look down at her desk's edge but it was a short-lived action, because the second her eyes left his, his hand lifted up to her chin and pulled her back towards him, forcing her to stare into his eyes once more.

"This is how you treat me despite how good I had you feeling last weekend," he continued. "Despite how good your pussy felt wrapped around my dick."

"K-Kalmon, what happened between us was a mistake."

Her words made him glare down at her, but his touch on her chin remained. Instead of spazzing out on her, he decided to hear her reasoning behind their supposed mistake.

"You clearly have a woman that is still in love with you and I'm not about to— Kalmon, what are you doing?"

"Keep talking. I'm listening."

"How can I keep talking when you're—"

"When I'm what?" he asked her, curiously.

Azia looked down at where he was now; on his knees, between her thighs and currently rubbing his hands up her legs like nothing was wrong; as if she wasn't trying to convince him of how them being together couldn't happen anymore.

"Kalmon, we can't."

He was currently reaching for her panties underneath her skirt and pulling them down her thighs.

"Says who?"

"I do," she confirmed, seeing the lust growing within him. "You have an ex that happens to be my best friend's cousin. An ex that clearly still wants you, and I don't want those type of problems."

"I don't give a fuck about her," he responded, looking at her black lace panties that were now by her ankles. He could see a slight wetness on them, telling him exactly what he already knew. She wanted him. "She's nothing to me."

"If she's nothing to you, why do you still have her number?"

He couldn't help but smile at how observant she was. He liked it.

"Cause she's my ex," he replied with a shrug, gazing up at her. "But if it's making you jealous baby, then by all means I'll block her number."

"That's not what I'm saying, Kalmon."

"Then what the fuck are you saying?" he asked, deciding to end their back and forth situation. "I heard you call what you and I did a mistake, when we both know that shit ain't true. I also heard you talk to me about my ex being your best friend's cousin, which I don't give a fuck about. Who I give a fuck about is standing right in front of me, wet as fuck for me right now and I intend to have her right here, right now before I take her home and fuck her for the rest of the day. That's all I give a fuck about."

Azia watched as he got up from his knees and stood tall in front of her. Her eyes refused to tear away from his and the fact that he had mentioned having her, had only turned her on even more. She had been turned on for this man from the second she laid eyes on him sitting by her desk, but she tried everything in her power to convince herself that she wasn't horny for him. It was the biggest lie though. She heard him say the word 'fuck' too many times in the last minute for her not to be turned on for him.

"I didn't take your number because I genuinely forgot," he informed her. "But best believe you don't have to worry about me forgetting that shit again. Even if I have to memorize it by heart then I'll do that, no doubt. The only thing you need to worry about is us. Who am I with right now?"

Azia looked at him as he took off his blazer, without breaking eye contact with her. But when she failed to answer him right away, he repeated his question with a tense stare.

"Who am I with right now, Azia?" he asked, chucking his blazer onto her desk before stepping forward to position himself directly in front of her again.

"Me," she said with a sigh. "Mainly because you refuse to leave my office."

Kalmon quickly grabbed her throat before stating, "Lose the fuckin' attitude."

"Or what?" She challenged him with a helpless grin.

The words *'or what'* turned out to be two words that Azia lowkey wished she had uttered much sooner.

"Uhhhhhmmhh!"

"See what happens when you talk all that... all that shit?"

The strokes she was receiving right now couldn't be normal. They just couldn't be. His dick had entered her passage and was now providing her with strokes that blew her mind away. He did it so effortlessly too.

"Mhhhhhhhh!"

Faster and deeper he pumped inside her. She could feel her walls contracting around his shaft with each movement and it only sent her mind into a frenzy. It wasn't fair how good he could fuck her. It wasn't fair how the slight curve in his dick could reach all her right spots.

"This is what happens when you talk all that mothafuckin' shit, Azia," he groaned in her ear as his pounds within her tightness continued.

"I'm... I'm s-sorryyyy, ahhhhmmmh!" She buried her head back between his neck to muffle her moans. Having the entire office hear how Kalmon was making her feel wasn't in her plans at all.

"Sorry just ain't gonna cut it. So keep taking this dick while I consider your apology."

"Mmmmmh!" Her muffled moans continued to sound.

Back and forth his shaft went within her. She couldn't even run from it even if she wanted to. He had both her legs locked around his clothed torso, keeping her right where he wanted her. Keeping her right in the perfect spot so he could hit her spot perfectly each thrust. Seeing the upper half of his clothed body, made her wetness run faster down her thighs as they continued to fuck. It must have been the fact that they were doing this in her office when they really weren't supposed to, that turned her on even more. And seeing Kalmon still with his open shirt on, reminded her of that fact. They were playing with danger because anyone could come in right now, but that only excited Azia further.

"Tell me how much you think we're a mistake again, Azia," he ordered, pulling her away from his neck and pushing her all the way down so that her back was now pressed against her desk, while he still slid in and out of her. During their love session, Kalmon managed to unbutton her shirt, exposing her black lace bra. It was a sight that made him want to cum already, but he kept his composure.

"We're no—we're... oh shit." Her whimpers and moans started to heighten and she quickly covered her mouth to silence herself.

"Uh-uh, don't get all shy and quiet now. Tell me, Azia. I wanna hear your ass tell me about our mistake. Now."

She slowly uncovered her mouth, feeling her body vibrate with each time that he filled her up. It's like she could feel him filling her up in every single part of her body; every part of her soul. It all felt too good to want to ever stop.

"We're no-we're not a mistake."

"Ex-fuckin'-actly," he confirmed, pausing mid-stroke inside her warm cave. "The only mistake you made was thinking I was about to let you go. You belong to me now, Azia."

He started pumping in and out of her again and Azia could feel her climax drawing in at any moment now. The more she looked up at him, the more she realized how serious he was being. She belonged to him.

CHAPTER 12

"How are things at the bakery, sis?"

"Good," Iman replied. "I honestly can't complain. As long as people keep loving cakes, then business will stay booming."

Iman had always had a passion for baking. It was something that her auntie taught her from the young age of ten, and once learning how to bake cakes and pies, it became second nature to her. It wasn't until she got older that she truly realized baking was her true calling and passion. A passion that she wanted to be able to make a living from. The idea of owning her own bakery was something that came to her in high school. From that day onward, Iman made it a priority to go through the right steps to have her shop. Now at the edge of twenty-seven, Iman had her own bakery.

Iman's *House of Treats* was the name of the bakery and it was located in downtown Manhattan. It was a popular spot with young people who were eager to try new cupcakes and other delicious treats. Iman's *House of Treats* not only served cupcakes, but waffles, pancakes, milkshakes and other sweet deserts. Iman baked when she had the time to, but because of how popular her bakery had become over the last year, she had to also manage the bakery. Trying to manage it while also trying to bake wasn't an easy task, which is why Iman hired a great team of skilled bakers who could bake as well as her and respected her wholeheartedly.

She could have just hired someone to manage the shop, but because it was her baby and only a year old, she'd rather be the one to manage it before trusting someone else to handle it. For now, she would remain the manager and hire a team to bake tasty treats.

"That's real good to hear," Athena said. "I don't tell you this enough, but I really am proud of you for starting your own bakery, sis. You had a dream and you worked hard to achieve it."

Iman grinned at her sister's words, placing her phone closer to her ear as she rested against her chair.

"Thank you so much, sis. I really do appreciate hearing that. Especially coming from you."

"No problem. It's nothing but the truth."

Iman's eyes scanned over the new cake recipe sitting on her desk in front of her before deciding to change the subject of the conversation she was having with Athena.

"How's my nephew?"

"He's good," Athena voiced. "At pre-school right now."

"I need to come visit you guys soon. It's been too long."

"It has but I get that you're busy with the shop and everything," Athena responded.

"I miss you guys though," Iman stated with a light sigh. "I'll be over sometime this week for sure."

"That sounds good. Athan's been missing his auntie."

"Awww and I've been missing him even more," Iman commented.

"I'm free whenever this week so just hit me up when you're ready."

"Alrightie, I sure will…"

Iman's words trailed off when she noticed who had stepped into the doorway of her office.

"Oh, hey Ke—"

But when he put a finger to his lips and shook his head at her, Iman decided not to make his presence known to her sister.

"What is it, Iman?" The worry in Athena's voice could not be masked.

"Oh nothing," Iman said, watching him confidently stride into her office. "I was just about to tell you about Azia working at Howard Enterprises. But you already knew that."

"Oh yeah, you said she's the marketing director at the company, right? Baby girl's making serious coins indeed."

"Yes she is," Iman agreed with a light chuckle. "Anyway, I gotta go now sis. I'll speak to you later though."

"Bye sis. Love you."

"Love you more," Iman concluded before hanging up the phone and looking over at the man that was now admiring the artwork hanging on her peach office walls. Artwork that was a painted portrait of Iman. She had gotten it from a friend last week who decided to paint it free of charge, but because of how great the painting was, Iman made sure to give her homeboy a payment for his talented work.

"This is fire," he spoke up before turning to look at her. "Looks exactly like you too."

Iman watched the way his lips curved into a smile and she found herself helplessly smiling back.

"It's good to see you, Keon."

"It's good to see you, Iman," he replied. "I didn't want you telling Athena I was here 'cause I wanted to surprise her with red—"

"Red velvet cupcakes," Iman knowingly stated, finishing off his sentence for him.

Almost every single week of the month, Keon came into Iman's *House of Treats* and bought the same batch of red velvet cupcakes. The red velvet cupcakes that happened to be Athena's favorite type of cupcake flavor.

"How could I ever forget you love surprising her with them? You're here like every week."

"Yeah, she loves them so much, but tries to act like she doesn't. We both know that's bullshit though."

"Yeah," Iman said with a nod, knowing fully well that if Athena had to choose between real food and red velvet cupcakes, she would choose the cupcakes every single time.

Iman got up from her seat and announced, "Let me get those packed for you."

Another thing that Iman knew was how Keon only liked her serving him, and no one else, which is why he had come through the back to see where she was. No one questioned him about it because they knew he was family.

"That portrait really is fire," Keon commented again once they were in the main shop and by the main checkout area.

Iman glanced up from the cupcakes she was packaging to see Keon's hard stare on her. She felt butterflies fly lightly in her stomach, but she quickly repressed them and focused on packaging his order.

"Thanks. I really like it too."

"Damn right you should," he voiced. "The painter really captured every feature of your face. It's beautiful."

Iman decided to take a risk by looking back up at him, only for her to lowkey regret it because the butterflies in her stomach started flying once again. Only this time, they were much stronger.

Staring into his brown eyes made Iman remember how handsome this man truly was. It wasn't something that she had actually forgotten; she just tried not to think about it too much. But forgetting was the very last thing on her mind as she stared up at him.

Keon Howard stood at 6'2 with deep-set chocolate brown eyes that sat below thick brows. His light beige skin coated his exterior and those lips of his looked like the softest, moistest lips Iman had ever laid eyes on. His light mustache bordered his full lips and along his jawline was a very light, smooth beard. And on his head sat waves in a ripple-like pattern, suiting the frame of his head well. He was currently dressed in an all-black tracksuit; the color black suiting him wonderfully.

"Thank you," she told him, now bagging his packaged baked goods.

"No, thank you for this store. Because of you I can treat my girl with her favorite cupcakes."

Iman simply smiled and served him with the cupcakes. When he paid and said his goodbyes, Iman watched him leave the shop before heading back to her office to look over her new cake recipe as she had been doing while on the phone with her sister.

Lowkey, Iman wished she had a man as attentive as Keon Howard. He really cared for her sister and over the past few years that they had been together, Iman never heard Athena complain. She was happy her sister had found her perfect man. She remembered the day that Athena and Keon met because it was the same day that Iman had met him too. As a matter of fact, Keon had been the one to approach Iman first at a kickback hosted by a mutual friend of Iman and Keon. He noticed her sitting by herself and came up to her. Then they talked for a while before Athena came along, finally arriving at the kickback after Iman had waited hours for her. When Iman saw the way that her younger sister's eyes twinkled as she stared at Keon, she knew right then and there that was Athena's man. Athena didn't play about what she wanted and being the good older sister that she was, Iman stepped out of the way and allowed Athena to do her thing.

Now three years later and they were still a perfect couple. They were real life couple goals. Something Iman hoped to have one day, but for now, she would stay focused on her business and doing her. That's all that truly mattered to her.

* * *

"So 50's paid his fee and wants roughly about 100 guests on that night."

Diamond's missing you already.

Send.

Kalmon looked up at the man he put in charge of his casino, six months ago, Caesar Gibson. A man that had proven his loyalty to Kalmon and had become someone he knew could manage his casino well.

"It's about to be a really big night, boss," Caesar stated. "More publicity for the casino which means more revenue."

Kalmon nodded before this attention went down to his vibrating phone.

Diamond's missing me? Or her owner?

Azia.

Maybe her owner too, he typed back, smirking to himself before looking back up at Caesar who was still standing in front of his desk.

"Is that all?"

Caesar stared down at his iPad before shaking his head.

"50 also wants us to provide unlimited bottles of his drink, Lechemin Du Roi, all night to his guests. Free of charge."

"This nigga sure is asking for a lot," Kalmon commented with his eyes glued down to his bright screen. Three dots had shown up in the chat he had open with Azia and he was waiting on her response to come through.

Azia: *I think he's definitely missing me.*

Azia: *Tell Diamond's owner, I'm missing him too.*

"Well his fee definitely makes up for it," Caesar responded with a light shrug.

Thinking about 50 Cent's fee to rent out Kalmon's casino for his birthday next month made Kalmon ease up his irritation a little bit. The rapper and actor 50 Cent had sought out Kalmon's casino because he wanted to have a casino themed birthday in the best casino in the whole city. So what better place to have it in other than Kalmon's establishment?

"True," Kalmon spoke up with a nod before typing back to Azia.

Kalmon: *That's what I like to hear.*

"It's going to be a good night though, boss. Everyone's looking forward to it. The team's 100% ready for that night."

"Great. Let everyone know they're allowed to bring a plus one on that night."

"Okay, I'll let them know."

"Who you bringing? Your girl?" Kalmon gave his manager an intrigued look.

"Yeah," Caesar confirmed with a small smile. "She likes partying, so this is just her kinda scene."

"Well that's good 'cause I'll finally get to meet the wife of my best manager."

One thing that Kalmon always made sure of was knowing everything important there was to know about the people he hired to work for him. He knew about Caesar having a wife of two years and a daughter on the way. Knowing that he had a family that depended on him only made Kalmon feel more inclined to have him managing the casino. He respected men who provided for their families because he could strongly relate.

"We're both really looking forward to it, boss."

A few hours later, Kalmon was done at the casino and headed home to get ready for his date night with Azia. Tonight he was doing something out of his comfort zone, something that he hadn't even done for his ex.

Speaking of his ex, Kalmon was glad to know that Jahana hadn't bothered trying to get in touch with him. She couldn't even if she tried to because Kalmon changed his number so that she couldn't get in contact with him. He was done with her.

The only person who had his full attention was Azia Price. That's the only woman he wanted to be around constantly and treat properly. It was too early to be thinking about getting in relationship with her, but it wasn't something that he was completely knocking. For now, he just wanted things to continue to flow naturally between them.

"Mmmm. Kalmon, this tastes really good. Let me se—"

"Uh-uh," Kalmon cut her off, slapping her hand away. "No peeking."

Azia pouted, sadly.

"Open up," he ordered. But when Azia refused to open up for him completely, he decided to sweeten her up. "Please, Zi. For me."

Azia grinned, showing off her pearly whites before doing as he asked and opening up her mouth for him. He placed the fork into her mouth and she ate off it. The rich, flavorful food settled in her mouth, firing up her taste buds and making her feel greatly satisfied.

"This is delicious. Oh my," she said as she chewed away.

"Good, right?"

"Hell yeah! What is that? I taste salmon for sure and…sweet chilli?"

Kalmon looked at the silk blindfold covering her eyes and could tell that she badly wanted to see her meal. She had already tried to take off the blindfold once, but he stopped her right in her tracks. He decided to put her out of her misery and removed the blindfold off her eyes, giving her back her sight.

Azia's eyes popped open and she looked over at Kalmon briefly before looking at the plate sitting below her.

"I was right!" she exclaimed in a cheerful tone. "It is salmon."

She reached for the fork that Kalmon was holding and began to eat the meal without his help.

"This is bomb," she said between her bites.

Kalmon had cooked salmon, white rice and vegetables on the side. The salmon had been seasoned and cooked well, telling Azia that this man knew how to throw down in the kitchen. It was a simple meal, but he had managed to make it taste like the greatest meal ever.

"I'm glad you like it," he said, reaching for his glass of champagne and lifting it to his mouth while keeping his eyes locked on her.

"So you proved yourself," Azia spoke up further, taking a break from her meal to talk to him. "You can cook."

"Told you," he replied, taking a piece of his salmon with his fork and eating it.

"I think you should do this more often," she suggested. "I want to see what else you can cook."

"And if I do that what will you be giving me in return?"

Azia let out a light giggle.

"Who said anything about me giving you anything in return?"

"Oh, so you just want to use my free cooking services, is that it?" His left brow arched at her.

"No, no," she said with a few more giggles. "What you get in return is a happy woman and a happy mouth who gets to try all of your amazing cooking."

"Oh, a happy mouth huh?"

The lust that she could see flashing in his eyes made her heart flutter, but instead of saying anything more to him, she shot him a sexy grin before continuing to eat her meal.

A few minutes later, they were both done with their meals and Azia insisted on washing the dishes, even though Kalmon told her not to worry about it. So while she washed, he watched her and dried their plates.

Azia barely said a word, but she didn't have to because the tension growing between them was undeniable. When she finally finished washing the dishes and Kalmon was drying the last one, she leaned against the sink and decided to just watch him without saying a word.

"What's on your mind?" he asked her, looking from her to the clean dish that he was now placing on the rack.

"Oh nothing," she began. "I'm just thinking."

"About?" Kalmon placed the towel to the side and turned his entire body around to face her.

"About…us," Azia admitted, gazing up at him.

"What about us?" he queried, inching closer towards her.

"Just thinking about how I enjoyed spending time with you tonight."

"I enjoyed spending time with you tonight too," he revealed, placing a hand to her waist and drawing her nearer to him. "But no one said anything about tonight being over between us."

Azia felt his other hand land on the side of her waist and she was directly in front of him while he leaned against the countertop. He then wrapped his arms around her and Azia loved how small she felt in his arms. He was so tall and mighty, towering over her and she absolutely adored it.

Before she knew it, their lips had joined and they were now kissing away like two passionate lovers, hungry to get a sweet taste of one another like they hadn't just had a meal. It didn't take long for Azia to be lifted onto the marble countertop and for Kalmon to be positioned in the center of her open thighs.

He broke their lips apart and looked down so that he could clearly see the bottom of her black dress. Then he started lifting it up, but the moment he started, the sound of barking filled the room and Azia looked behind Kalmon only to laugh at who had just barked.

"Ah shit," Kalmon groaned. "Someone's up from their nap and grumpy as hell."

Kalmon turned around to look at the teacup yorkie poo who was now running over to where they were in the kitchen.

"Hey Diamond," Azia greeted her.

"Zi and I are kinda in the middle of something right now, D. So unless you tryna see me eat this pussy, I suggest you get gone."

Azia suddenly gasped at his remark before letting out a loud laugh and playfully hitting his hard chest.

"She can stay if she wants to," Azia preached.

"Uh-uh, no she can't," Kalmon retorted, focusing back on lifting up Azia's dress before changing his mind. "Matter of fact, she ain't even gotta leave, we're leaving."

Kalmon then lifted Azia off the kitchen counter and wrapped her thighs around his torso, leading the way out of the kitchen and upstairs to his bedroom.

Azia only found herself chuckling more and more as Diamond trailed along behind Kalmon.

"D, I ain't about to tell you again. You wanna sleep in your cold ass cage tonight or your warm comfy bed?" Kalmon asked her while still leading the way up the stairs with Azia on him. He couldn't see Diamond following him, but he could hear her light steps and feel her movement behind him.

Once they reached the top of the stairs, Kalmon let Azia back down on her feet before looking down his staircase only to see Diamond stationary on the middle step.

"That's what I thought," he said, knowingly. "Now take your ass back downstairs."

Diamond gave him one last look before doing as he asked and running back downstairs to her living space.

"She was only being friendly, Kalmon."

"No, she was being clingy," he explained, grabbing Azia's hand and leading her to his bedroom. "I know how she gets when she just wakes up and shit, wanting my attention but she can't have that right now because a different lady owns it tonight."

Azia watched as he switched on his lights and walked deeper into his bedroom.

"She must be one special lady to have all your attention tonight."

"Oh believe me, she is," Kalmon commented, turning around in his stance to look at her.

Tonight she looked even more beautiful than she usually did. Her brown hair was loosely curled, giving her hair slightly more volume and definition. She barely had on any make up, which he preferred and the black dress that she came dressed in for him, made his mind race with thoughts of all the nasty little things he wanted to do to her.

"One very special lady," Kalmon whispered as he edged closer towards her.

When he was directly in front of her, he bent low towards her neck and started pecking her warm skin while both his hands went to the straps of her dress.

Azia's eyes shut as she felt her dress slowly slide down her body, until it dropped to the floor, leaving her in nothing but her thong. His lips were still kissing on her flesh and she could feel her wetness soaking her underwear fabric quicker and quicker.

His large hands went to her breasts, cupping them gently before squeezing them tightly while his lips trailed down her neck.

Azia felt her breathing get heavy as his mouth kissed lower down her chest and his hands massaged her mounds. And just when she opened her eyes to look at him, he carried her over to his California king-sized bed.

"Kalmon."

By now, Azia was laying right in the center of his bed, right where he needed her to be. He silently watched her, while beginning to take off his t-shirt, followed by his jeans and boxers. Azia looked at him getting naked and internally moaned at how good his body looked. The sight of his abdominal and arm muscles flexing made her feel giddy. This man was truly perfection personified.

"What's wrong?"

"Nothing's wrong," she spoke up, her eyes widening as she took a glance at the lengthened treasure between his thighs.

"Don't lie to me."

She took a deep breath, staring into his heavenly eyes, before deciding to speak further. "I know this isn't the best time to bring this up but…" Her words trailed off as Kalmon climbed on the bed and positioned himself in the center of her thighs.

"But what?" He flashed a sexy smile her way, revealing his pearly whites. "Huh?"

"Well I wanted to know how you…" Her words trailed off once his soft lips wrapped around her left nipple. "How you feel about…us not letting everyone at work know our business?"

Azia had worked hard to be in the position she was in currently, and as much as she was feeling Kalmon, she didn't want to be the talk of the company because she was currently sleeping with her boss's son. And she didn't want Kalmon's secret admirers coming for her neck either.

Kalmon released his mouth from around her nipple and held her gaze.

"Are you scared of what my mom will think?"

"No. I'm more scared of what people at the company will say. You've been a trending topic since you arrived and I don't want the drama that will come if ladies find out that you and I are messing around."

"I hear that, but you don't have shit to worry about, Zi," he promised, pressing a kiss to her chest.

"I know, but this is my job, Kalmon. I just don't want any problems."

"And you won't. I got you," he concluded before placing his mouth back on her nipple and beginning to suck away like his life depended on it.

Azia found herself letting out low, sensual moans as his tongue did its magic on her nipple. He stayed focused on her left one first; sucking and licking it to complete hardness. He circled his tongue around her brown bud, using his saliva to coat it completely and giving it as much love as possible before he moved on to her right one and pleased it in the exact same way that he had done the first one.

Then he flattened his tongue against her skin, making a wet trail down her chest until he reached the top of her pink thong.

Azia watched with a bated breath as he slowly pulled off her thong, taking it down her thighs and all the way down to her ankles. Once he chucked it to the side, Kalmon leaned closer into her heavenly center, already loving the sight of her wet arousal flowing out her folds.

"I meant what I said, Zi," he announced. "You have nothing to worry about because I got you. It'll be our lil secret. A'ight?"

"Okay," she responded, observing him raise her thighs up on his shoulders.

Kalmon pushed his head further between her thighs and placed his entire mouth on her entrance; not wanting to waste time with getting to taste her sweet nectar.

Azia's back arched slightly off the bed as Kalmon ate her out in the best way. Her eyes stayed sealed on the sight of his lips sucking on her pussy with no hesitation. Sucking her like he was trying to snatch her soul, and at this point, Azia was convinced that he was doing exactly that. Then his tongue dived past her tightness and started darting back and forth inside her.

In. Out. In. Out.

"Ahhhh, shit."

His tongue thrusted within her, making her scrunch her face up because of the intense pleasure that he was making her feel already. It was too early for her to be feeling this good! Way too early, but here he had her mind blown as his tongue effortlessly fucked her.

Shit, what is he doing to me?

"Kal...mon, uh, fuck," she moaned, placing a hand to the back of his head to keep him exactly where he was.

She could hear him groan as his tongue kept pushing in and out of her before he stopped momentarily, only to bring his tongue out to massage against her warm folds. Then he dived back in, making sure to keep both his eyes stuck on hers, observing the sexy faces that she made as he devoured her like the amazing meal that she was. The meal that he would never get tired of having.

"Kalmon, ughhhhh!"

"That's right, baby," he whispered between his manoeuvres. "Ride my fuckin' face like you own this shit."

Her moans and whimpers only increased in volume as his tongue continued to work his magic on her intimate part, letting him know that he was doing exactly everything he needed to do and more. He absolutely loved the way she tasted, smelled and even the way her nectar was running out, glossing his beard. She was everything to him and all Kalmon wanted to be able to do was make her feel good. Making her feel good was what made him feel even better and for some strange reason, Kalmon was addicted to that feeling. He was becoming addicted to her.

CHAPTER 13

"So she lied," Nova stated with a frown. "What a bitch."

"Nova! That's your cousin," Azia replied with her mouth hung open.

"Nah fuck that! It's a free country, right? Let her say what she wants," Iman voiced before muttering, "It's the truth anyway."

Iman muttered under her breath, but both Azia and Nova had heard her, and they all giggled before reaching for their cocktails and taking a sip.

The besties were at their favorite bar in the city; the place where they got lit together and were able to catch up on their lives. Azia had just finished updating her girls about her current situation with Kalmon. How she confronted him about having a girlfriend and how he called Jahana in front of her on loudspeaker so that Azia could hear their entire conversation. Kalmon made sure that Jahana confirmed the fact that their relationship was over and made sure she knew that they were never getting back together.

"So you really are fucking with him then," Iman stated. "Who would have thought Azia would have bagged Kalmon Howard?"

"I haven't bagged him, we're just messing around."

"Messing around for now, then before you know it, one of you will catch feelings," Nova commented.

"And my money's on the woman who's getting her back blown."

Azia playfully rolled her eyes at Iman's comment before taking another sip of her cocktail.

"We're just having fun right now, that's all," she said once done sipping. "I don't have time to be catching feelings; my main focus is my career. I might not have made partner, but I'm not about to give up on my goals. I was given this job for a reason and I'm not about to risk it all. A relationship is the last thing on my mind right now."

"But aren't you kinda risking it all by sleeping with him?" Iman piped up.

"No, 'cause we've both agreed to keep our situation a secret," Azia explained. "No one knows about us at work and I'd rather it stay that way for now."

"You never know though," Nova chimed in. "One day you might just suddenly wake up and realize that this is the guy you want for the rest of your life and not care about who knows about you two. The same way I woke up and realized Caesar is the only man for me."

Nova began smiling to herself as she looked down at the silver diamond ring on her finger. The promise ring that Caesar had gifted her with last night, promising to always be her man.

Nova hadn't originally shown off her ring when meeting her girls. But she didn't need to because Iman spotted the sparkling ring five minutes into them sitting at the bar. At first Azia and Iman were worried that Nova had been proposed to, until she carefully explained what the ring actually was. Caesar had gifted a promise ring to her, promising to always remain by her side and to one day make her his wife.

"Has Caesar met your family yet, Nova?" Iman questioned her best friend with an intrigued look.

"No not yet," Nova replied, taking one last glance at her ring before looking directly at Iman who sat next to her.

"Are you planning to introduce him anytime soon?"

"The thought has crossed my mind, but I've been busy and so has he."

Iman simply shook her head, taking another sip of her cocktail before speaking up again, "Have you met any of his family?"

"No," Nova voiced with a straight face.

"Interesting," Iman commented.

"Interesting?" Nova's brows knotted at Iman's words. "What's so interesting about that?"

"It's interesting that he's given you a promise ring when you hardly know a damn thing about him. You haven't even met his mom."

"Excuse me?"

Nova's voice had gone up a few octaves, indicating to Azia the nasty turn this conversation was about to take. And she knew that she needed to step in to stop her best friends from engaging in a full-blown argument.

"Guys, let's just rela—"

"I'm just being honest, Nova," Iman responded with a light shrug. "You and Caesar have only known each other for a few months, and you haven't even met his family or friends. Hell, we haven't even met his ass yet! So how can he be so sure about marrying you when he barely knows you?"

"My relationship with Caesar is between Caesar and I. He's given me a promise ring because he loves and understands me. Something that you wouldn't understand because you haven't got a man, Iman."

Azia's mouth hung open as she looked at the seriousness plastered upon Nova's face after the words that she had just uttered. Azia was hoping that it was just a joke and Nova didn't actually mean what she said.

"Nova, you don't mean that," Azia said, praying that Nova was about to take back her rude comment.

"I sure do," Nova confirmed with a firm nod. "Maybe when you get your own man, you'll stop worrying about me and mine."

"Bitch fuck you and your man," Iman retorted, hurt deep down by Nova's comment. "No one cares about your relationship. I'm just telling you like it is. You barely know this guy and here he is, dropping promise rings on you? A promise ring? What are you? Sixteen?" Iman let out a bitter laugh. "He never takes you out in public, Nova. Every single date you've told us about, he's had you in a room, locked away from everyone else. How can a man promise to marry you one day when he doesn't even have the balls to be seen with you in public? When he keeps you away from spending time with your friends? Seems like he's just trying to sweeten you up, and you being the gullible little person that you are, you're eating all this shit up."

"Iman stop it. Please," Azia pleaded with her friend, trying her hardest to somehow take control of this situation, but failing miserably. Both of her best friends were going at it and she really didn't know what to do. Mostly because this argument had come completely out of the blue.

Nova didn't like how Iman's words were making sense. Caesar had never taken her out on a public date. At first, she thought nothing of it because she enjoyed spending quality time with her man, but now that Iman brought it up, had Nova feeling some type of way.

"If it wasn't for the fact that you and I go way back, I swear I would fuck you up right now," Nova fumed. "I always thought you had my best interests at heart and me telling you about my relationship with Caesar was a way of us bonding and connecting as best friends. But I see now that I was wrong. You're nothing but a jealous, judgmental bitch."

"If I'm a jealous bitch then you must be a silly one for letting this man sell you dreams. Wake up and smell the roses, Nova!" Iman waved her hands in the air. "He's not ever going to marry you."

Without even hesitating, Nova reached for her glass and threw its remaining contents on Iman, resulting in Iman gasping with horror at her now wet garments, and before she could even try to retaliate, Nova left her seat and was leaving the bar.

"Nova!" Azia exclaimed with annoyance. "What the hell just happened?" she was asking herself, but Iman chose to respond while wiping her wet eyes with her hands.

"Some friend she is!"

Azia quickly reached for the napkins that the male bartender was now passing their way and passed them over to Iman.

"She can't handle the truth so this is how she acts!" Iman yelled while dabbing her face dry. "I guess our friendship over."

"Iman, you don't mean that shit."

"Yes I do! I can't be friends with someone who neglects her friends for her man and expects to not be called out on her so-called relationship. Then she has the audacity to throw a drink on me? Yeah, I don't think I want anything to do with her anymore."

"Iman, you did come on strong when talking about her relationship with Caesar and her not meeting his family or friends yet."

"Yeah, but was I wrong?" Iman questioned Azia. "He's given her a ring without even bothering to meet her family or friends. Shit just don't make sense. Mark my words, that man isn't as perfect as Nova believes he is and when she figures it out, I won't be the one consoling her."

How things had turned so ugly between her two best friends made Azia feel depressed. Iman definitely came on strong, but she had made some valid points; Azia couldn't deny that. However, she didn't want to see her squad break up because of Nova's relationship with her man. It just wasn't right to Azia and she knew that getting her friends to reconcile would have to be her priority from this day forward.

CHAPTER 14

FIVE DAYS LATER

"They're still not talking?"

"No mom, they're not. And I really don't know what to do."

Azia let out a frustrated sigh as she contemplated about the past few days. She had tried to get her best friends to agree to meet up so that they could end their disagreement, but neither of them complied. They were both being stubborn as hell and it pained Azia to see. Iman and Nova were her two best friends and she truly appreciated their friendship. They had been there for her during times when she felt like she had no one else. Azia might have been the only child of her parents, but to her Iman and Nova were her sisters.

"Maybe the best thing for you to do is to give them some space, ZiZi," Rivera advised her daughter. "Make them come to the realization that they miss each other and don't wanna be at odds anymore by themselves. 'Cause if you keep trying to force them to be friends once again, it might just push them further apart."

"I miss my friends though, mom. I just want everything to be back to normal. This is stupid. They shouldn't be arguing over Nova's man."

"They shouldn't be but they are," Rivera reminded her gently. "As their friend I think it's best you try to remain as neutral as possible and pray that sooner than later they decide to sort things out. They were the ones that made the conscious decision to get themselves into the argument, so they must be the ones to make the conscious decision to make up."

"I hear you, mommy. Thank you for listening to me and giving such great advice as always."

"Anytime, ZiZi. You know mommy's got you."

After speaking to her mother on the phone, Azia decided to give her apartment a deep clean. It was officially the weekend and Azia was happy to be able to stay in the comfort of her home without worrying about going out anywhere. She was a homebody at heart and loved being at home so she could order some food and binge watch an interesting Netflix series.

Ding!

She heard her phone sound off while laying her new bed sheets down and walked over to her bedside table to take a peek at it.

It's been too long.

When am I seeing you?

Nahmir.

Azia simply cleared his text message notification from her screen and placed her phone back on the table.

For the past few days, Nahmir had been pressing her hard. Texting her about wanting to see her and missing her badly. It was funny to her because before Kalmon confirmed his dead relationship with his ex, Azia was actually entertaining Nahmir and making herself believe that she was actually interested in messing around with him again. But now that Kalmon was the man dominating the space between her thighs most nights, the thought of being with anyone else but him wasn't something that appeased her. She found it strange too, because she and Kalmon didn't have a title on their situation but here she was, being loyal to him.

After she was done cleaning her bedroom, her bathroom, her living room and kitchen, Azia was officially tired. And the only thing that she could physically bring herself to do was get under her fresh new bed covers and take a lovely Saturday nap. So that's exactly what she did.

Knock! Knock!

It was only seven hours later that she woke up to the loud sound of knocking on her front door. The knocking caught her off guard completely but instead of rushing to the door, she reached to the side table for her phone to see that the time was. 9pm.

Shit. Did I really sleep that long?

She didn't believe she was that tired. In her mind, a quick two-hour power nap would do and she would carry on with the rest of her weekend. However, she had basically slept her entire Saturday away.

Knock! Knock!

More knocks sounded, but instead of rushing to see who was at the door, Azia got out of bed to head to her bathroom; peeing quickly and taking a look at her reflection to see if she was decent. She took her head scarf off her head and fixed her hair by brushing it straight. When she finished she put her robe on and rushed to the front door only to frown when she was greeted to the face of...

"Nahmir?"

"Hey," he greeted her warmly. "You weren't answering my texts so I figured I'd come 'round to check on you. I like your hair."

Azia crossed her arms in front of her and looked at him with a skeptical eye. She appreciated the compliment on her new hairstyle, which was a frontal lace blonde wig with dark roots, suiting her golden honey complexion perfectly. But what she didn't appreciate was the fact that he had arrived on her doorstep, because she wasn't prepared to see him today, or anyone for that matter. However, Azia knew that he wasn't really checking up on her. What he was really trying to check up on was the private part that lived between her thighs. A private part that wasn't his to access anymore.

"Can I come in?"

Despite the slight reluctance she felt, she decided to let him in only because he had come all this way. Nahmir resided in Queens, which was just over thirty minutes away by car from Azia's home. It wasn't extremely long, but it was still a journey, which is why she felt more inclined to let him in.

"I ain't heard from you in a minute; got me thinking I did something wrong."

Azia watched the way his lips moved as he spoke and the way he had become so comfortably seated on her couch. As she looked at him more and more, she realized that she didn't feel that same attraction that she used to feel for him.

Nahmir Sterling wasn't an ugly guy in the slightest way. He had the smoothest looking rich mink skin, hooded brown eyes, thick lips and an athletic, tall frame. Ugly couldn't be a word to describe him at all.

"You didn't do anything wrong," Azia assured him in a quiet tone.

Nahmir looked over at her suspiciously. For starters, he didn't like the fact that she had decided to sit on the opposite couch instead of next to him, and he didn't like the fact that she was constantly using her hands to keep her robe covering her body like he hadn't seen everything there was to see many times before. Even the way her eyes drifted away from his from time to time had him feeling unimportant like she had somewhere else to be or something better to do.

"So why'd you ghost on me?" he queried, leaning forward so he could get a better look of that pretty face he hadn't gotten a chance to see in what felt like forever.

"I've been busy," she said. "With work and…" Azia took a mental pause to debate with herself if bringing up the real reason why she never hit Nahmir up anymore was a smart option. "To be honest with you Nahmir, I'm kinda seeing someone else right now."

He blinked rapidly at her, taken aback by what she had just said.

"Oh, really?" he asked with surprise. A part of him wanted to snap on her but he quickly repressed those negative feelings away. "Well I didn't expect you to say that."

"I know, I know. I wasn't going to say anything at first, but I don't want you to think I'm stringing you along. This new situation I'm in is different and even though I'm not in a relationship, I have to be honest and say that I am more interested in my current situation than I was with you. That's why I haven't hit you back yet."

Azia expected him to respond back straight away but when he just kept on staring at her blankly, she decided to speak up again. This time apologizing.

"Nahmir, I'm so sorry."

"Why are you apologizing?" he asked her with a confused look before chuckling lightly. "I should be the one apologizing, hitting you up constantly and showing up at your crib unannounced. You and I were never in a relationship and we never talked about being exclusive."

"So, you're not mad?"

"Nah, nah never that beautiful. I'm cool. I appreciate you being honest with me rather than letting me believe I'd done something wrong."

Azia let out the breath she had been holding and gave him a small smile which he instantly returned.

"At the end of the day, your happiness is key. And I'm happy you've found someone who really interests you Azia, even if that person isn't me."

Azia's smile only grew bigger as her eyes stayed sealed on his. She was grateful that he was being so understanding about her ending things between them and not turning this into an unnecessary argument.

"Who would have thought Azia would be in love?"

She let out a light chuckle.

"Oh no, I'm not in love. I'm just enjoying the time I'm spending with this guy, that's all."

"Well like I said before, as long as you're happy then I'm happy."

"Thank you so much for understanding, Nahmir. Maybe you and I can remain friends?"

"Sure," he said with a nod. "Friends is cool. I just hope your new man approves."

Azia playfully rolled her eyes at him. Kalmon wasn't her man but she couldn't be bothered to correct Nahmir on his comment. She knew he was calling Kalmon her man in a joking way after she had already confirmed not being in a relationship.

"Maybe one day I'll meet the lucky guy," Nahmir commented, leaning back against her couch.

"Maybe," Azia stated meekly, not really a fan of two men that she'd messed with meeting up and her having to introduce them to one another. How would it even go?

Oh, hey Kalmon, this is Nahmir. The guy who used to blow my back out before you did. He's a nice guy, not too bad in bed but gets leg cramps easily.

And Nahmir, this is Kalmon. The guy currently breaking my back out in five different places every night he can get his hands on me. He's also a demon with that tongue of his, using it to drive me insane whenever he eats my pus—

Azia quickly shook the thought of introductions out of her head. That was definitely something she never wanted to happen. There was no reason for them to ever meet. It would be pointless and awkward for Azia to have to introdu—

Knock! Knock!

"Expecting company?" Nahmir questioned her while looking across at her front door. Azia simply shook her head no while getting up from her seat and walking over to the door.

It was 9:30pm on a Saturday. A Saturday that she had planned to spend all by herself until the arrival of an unexpected guest, Nahmir. Now there was another unexpected arrival at her door?

Once at the door, she opened it and was instantly greeted to those enchanting brown irises of his. Those irises that were gazing back at her like he wanted to eat her up. And eat her up was exactly what he wanted to do, especially seeing her come to the door in her black silk robe and her new blonde hair.

"Azia, you good?"

Eating her up like his favorite desert was exactly what he intended to do until he heard a deep voice emerge from behind her. Then he took a glance into her apartment and spotted the figure sitting on her gray couch. An emotion that he never felt instantly filled his body.

Jealousy.

CHAPTER 15

"Aren't you going to ask me who that was?"

"No."

"No?"

"No," Kalmon repeated, giving her an emotionless stare. "That nigga ain't important, so why would I ask?"

Azia looked over at him without saying a word and then took a bite of her chow mein.

When she let him in and introduced him to Nahmir, Nahmir openly greeted him whereas Kalmon said nothing. He didn't offer him a hi, hello or anything. Not even a simple nod.

Kalmon just came straight into her apartment, and went into her kitchen where he began finding cutlery for the Chinese takeout he brought for her, without saying a single word. Now that Nahmir was gone and Azia was eating the food he brought for her, he was talking.

"I know you've fucked him."

Azia felt her noodle get stuck in her throat and she coughed powerfully to get it back up before reaching ahead for her Snapple juice drink. Once taking a sip from it, she looked up at him only to see the amusement dancing in his eyes.

"And how do you think you know that?"

"Don't play with me," he lightly warned her. "I saw the way he was looking at you and coming over at this time? Yeah he was definitely tryna get some action."

"And how do you know he didn't get any?" Azia taunted him.

"Cause you damn sure ain't about to let that nigga touch you ever again when you know you belong to me."

Azia felt her cheeks quickly get hot and her eyes stayed fixed on him. Ignoring his comment, she chose to question him.

"So what's your reason for coming over at this time?"

Kalmon flashed her a toothy smile before saying, "I wanted to see you."

"You wanted to see me?"

"Yeah."

"No, you just wanted to fuck," she bluntly told him while twirling noodles onto her fork and lifting it to her mouth. "And so do I, so you're lucky."

"Oh I'm the lucky one?"

"Yup," she concluded and then ate off her fork while watching him.

"Five days without that smart-ass mouth of yours. Yeah, I've definitely missed you."

He hadn't been at *Howard Enterprises* all week and their text messages had been short conversations, mostly of them asking each other how they were. She definitely missed him too, if not more, but she wasn't about to admit that to him.

"Nahmir and I used to mess around, but I officially ended things with him today."

"Good to hear," Kalmon replied. "No need for me to intervene then."

"Intervene?"

"Yup. 'Cause if you hadn't ended things with the nigga then best believe I would have done it for you."

"Done it for me how?"

"That's nothing you need to worry about because you've done it all by yourself, Azia. Now he knows not to try to press you for sex. There's only one person who gets to do that and he's sitting right in front of you."

"You really do believe that I belong to you and no one else," she stated, placing her empty takeaway box on the coffee table in front.

"Tell me you don't," he demanded with a firm look.

"I don't. Azia Price belongs to me, myself and I."

"Well if you don't belong to me, tell me why I know how wet you're getting as you've been sitting across from me, eating your food?" Azia's heart skipped a beat at his question.

"Why have your nipples gotten so hard, Azia?" She felt her mouth get dry. "I haven't even touched you yet and here you are, hot and bothered for me."

She lowkey hated how right he was. There wasn't a single lie in the words he had just uttered.

"But I gotta be honest with you, Zi, you and this new blonde hair have me just as hot and bothered for you too. Fuck," he cursed as he bit his lips, admiring her hair once again. Azia helplessly smiled, feeling gassed at his reaction to her new hair. She then got up and made her way to where he sat, standing in front of his open legs and slowly untying her robe, revealing her navy vest top and matching panties.

Kalmon watched with excitement as her robe dropped to the floor and she lowered herself onto his lap, frontwards. He placed his hands on her waist and smiled up at her once he clearly noticed the look in her eyes; the look that told him that she wanted him. And as Azia sat on his lap, she could feel how bad he wanted her too with his arousal poking her middle.

Their lips joined and their heated kiss commenced. Tongues syncing and their hands roaming each other's bodies. They had missed each other this past week and they were both ready to show each other just how much.

Their first session of the night happened right on her couch before they ended up in her bedroom for their second. And after their love making, Azia was in his arms with his dick still nested up inside her. He hadn't pulled out yet and she hadn't been bothered to slide off him. It felt quite nice with him still within her walls, keeping them connected. They were laying on their sides, with Kalmon positioned behind her.

"You must want me to kill every nigga that tries to make a move at you."

Azia let out a soft gasp before responding, "Kill? Kalmon, that's too extreme."

He said some of the wildest stuff sometimes, but she was quickly getting used to it.

"No, what's extreme is the shit you did while riding me on your couch," he whispered in her ear. "Caressing my balls while riding me? You're the one trying to kill me."

Azia giggled before sighing deeply. Kalmon kissed her cheek and neck a few times. Her sighing hadn't gone unnoticed and he was planning to address it but first he wanted to kiss up on her.

"What's on your mind, Zi?" he asked just after his last peck on her soft skin. He reached for her hand under the covers and their hands joined.

Azia was silent for a few seconds and then she spoke up.

"My girls aren't speaking and it's really annoying me."

"Iman and Nova?"

She nodded. Kalmon was aware of her best friends because she'd brought them up before. He met Iman a few times at the birthday parties of their nephew. And of course, he knew about Nova being Jahana's cousin because Azia told him.

"Why?"

"They got into some bullshit argument about Nova's man giving her a promise ring, promising to marry her one day. Iman brought up the fact that he hasn't met any of her friends or family. And then Nova snapped, insulting Iman for not having a man. She also threw a drink on her and..." Azia suddenly paused, coming to the realization that she was talking a lot. "I'm sorry, you probably don't even want to hear this shit right no—"

"Nah, of course I do baby," he cut her off. "Don't feel like you can't ever talk to me about your problems, because you can. I'm here for you. Always."

Hearing his kind words made happiness flow through her veins. It was great to hear him tell her that he was here for her and willing to listen to whatever she had to say. So Azia continued filling him in on what happened with Nova and Iman, including the advice her mother had given her. And when she was done, Kalmon gave her his two cents on the situation.

"What Iman said was harsh, but she does lowkey have a point. However, that still doesn't give her the right to make Nova feel bad about her relationship with her man. I hear what your mom was saying about letting them come to a conscious decision, but I think as their friend, it's important you sit them down one-on-one and get them to access the situation. You know them better than anyone else and you know how stubborn they are. Make them both see how unnecessary it is for them to be arguing over some shit that shouldn't affect their friendship. Iman needs to understand that love doesn't have a time stamp and even though Nova's dude hasn't met her parents or friends yet, that doesn't mean he doesn't care for Nova. Nova needs to put her foot down though and make that shit happen. If she really sees a future with this guy then she needs to introduce him to y'all because you're already part of her present and future."

Azia was astonished by his words and she turned her head to look at him, giving him shocked eyes.

"Damn."

"What?"

"You sound so sexy when you're giving advice Kal," she admitted with a smirk.

Kalmon simply grinned before sweetly pecking her lips.

"Thank you for the advice. I'm gonna do what you said and see how it goes."

"You're welcome. Don't worry, it'll work and you gon' have your friends talking in no time. Then you'll be able to tell them all about this"—he paused to peck her soft lips—"dick."

Azia chuckled heartily.

"Who said we would be talking about you? I'm looking forward to telling them about how I let Nahmir break my back one last time while leaving Kalmon knocking on my door."

"Oh I see you got jokes, huh?" he asked her. "You got jokes, huh Azia?"

Kalmon let go of her hand under the sheets, using it to tickle her stomach; one of her many ticklish spots.

"Nooooo. Kal stop. Nooooo," she pleaded with him while letting out an endless amount of laughter.

The pair of them continued talking and messing around until Kalmon came up with the suggestion of them hopping in Azia's shower together, which she willingly agreed to. Azia got prepared by placing her black shower cap on her head, protecting her hair from getting wet. Surprisingly she wasn't nervous about taking a shower with Kalmon, despite the fact that she'd never showered with a guy before. She was more so looking forward to it than shy.

Once they were both in, the warm water soaked both of their skin. Azia tried to reach for her soap and pink loofah but Kalmon beat her to it.

"I got you," he simply told her. "Just relax."

Azia watched him lather up her loofah before beginning to gently scrub her clean. Every part of her body he paid attention to, starting with her arms, upper chest then slowly down her body, being very attentive with her body like she was a precious object that he needed to be careful with.

Having him clean her was an act that she hadn't expected, but now that it was happening and she was loving it. She was loving every second of it and didn't want this moment to end so soon.

Then it was her turn to wash him. She took her extra time, paying attention to each part of his body, from his muscular chest, his arms, his back and down to the growing member between his thighs. The member that she gently stroked with her hands, resulting in his erection to grow.

"Fuck, Zi."

His eyes shut as he enjoyed the feel of her hand moving back and forth on his shaft, providing him with a deeply satisfying pleasure. But with that pleasure came the urge for him to have her.

Kalmon removed her hands from his dick before lifting her up and locking her thighs around his torso. Then he pushed her against the beige porcelain tiled wall and kissed into her neck.

"You're so perfect, Azia. So fuckin' perfect," he said as he pushed himself within her, inch by inch. "There's no one else I want but you."

"No one else?" she queried, feeling her walls tightening around him.

"No one else," he promised, easing out of her. "The same way you belong to me Zi"—Azia whimpered as he pounded into her, sending waves of ecstasy down her spine—"is the same way I belong to you. You have me, baby. You have me all the way."

Kalmon decided to stop talking, sealed his lips to hers and carried on his rhythmic movement between her thighs, muffling both their moans with their wet, sloppy kiss. And while they connected, all Azia could think about was how intense them having sex right now felt. He had basically admitted his feelings for her and Azia knew that she felt the same exact way. There was no other man she wanted but him. He had her all the way.

* * *

"So son, how are things?"

"Decent Pop, they're decent."

"But not good," Fontaine's knowing tone seeped through the exterior of Keon's Bugatti.

Keon was currently driving through the streets of Manhattan, making his way back home after being at the headquarters of his app development company. A company that he loved with all his heart and soul. He was glad that his company was doing so well when it wasn't even a year old yet.

"What did he do now?"

"It's not what he's done," Keon explained with one hand on the steering wheel as he drove and the other palming the back of his neck. "It's what he's failed to do... I just wish he'd be more vocal with me about our business and the moves he decides to suddenly make. I know he's the oldest, but a little heads up would be cool. It's like he sometimes forgets we're supposed to be a team, doing things together."

Finding out that Kalmon had bought out new warehouses to place product in wasn't a surprise to Keon. They moved a lot of product through the city and they never liked keeping things stationary for too long, but still they needed all the storage they could get. So he understood Kalmon's business move but he just would have preferred it if Kalmon had spoken to him like an actual partner would. But buying new warehouses wasn't the only thing that Kalmon had done independently. He also hired a few new faces in their drug sorting team, something Keon found out from Jahmai.

It just didn't sit right that he was finding out things from Jahmai, their cousin who they hired as their distributor. Jahmai was supposed to be finding out things from them, not the other way round.

"Have you tried talking to him about it?"

"He knows how I feel about him not including me in his ideas," Keon stated. "If I have to remind him once again then it's gonna be an issue between us."

"You know I don't like getting in the middle of you and Kalmon's business, unless I really have to. If I need to step in here then I will."

The fact that their father left them the family business meant that he trusted them enough to work together. Having Fontaine talk to his brother about something that wasn't even that significant just didn't sit right with Keon.

"Nah, it's cool Pop. It's not that deep. I'll talk to him myself."

At the end of the day, this was just something that needed to be discussed and handled between them. And Keon would make sure that Kalmon understood to treat him more like an equal and less like a little brother that needed to be told what to do and how to do it, or Keon would just have to take matters into his own hands.

Once making it home to his family, Keon was glad to see his girlfriend and son snuggled up together on the couch watching Athan's favorite film, Toy Story. Well it was more so Athena watching the film because Athan had fallen asleep. But the sight still warmed his heart none-theless.

"Pookie."

Athena smiled as she heard him call her by the nickname he had given her a few months into their relationship. He called her that because he said she was soft just like a pookie bear. Her hands were soft, her face and her booty that he loved rubbing on was soft too.

"Yes, Key?"

She turned from where she sat on the edge of their bed to see him standing over at her bedside.

"What do you think about us having another kid?"

Athena gave him a blank stare and said nothing in return.

"I mean, I know I said I wanted to put a ring on you before we have any more kids, but baby I want another kid," he explained. "It's not something that needs to happen straight away, I just wanted to get your thoughts on the matter."

Athena broke into a friendly smile.

"I'm all for it, honey. You want a big family and so do I," she responded. "I'm down 100%."

Keon felt his happiness cloud his thoughts and he jumped on the bed to be near her. Athena giggled once he grabbed her and pushed her back down to the bed while climbing on top of her.

"If you're 100% down then you're 100% willing to practice some baby making right now."

Athena looked up at him and bit her lips before slowly nodding.

"We can't though, Key," she whispered with regret.

"Why not?"

"It's that time of the month."

"Ahh damn," he voiced, annoyed he couldn't make love to his woman right now. "I've missed you though. It's been almost a week since we had sex."

"I know baby, but this is out of my control. I started this morning."

Keon nodded with understanding before he gave her forehead a gentle peck. Then he climbed off her and lay beside her.

"I know exactly how to make you feel better though," Athena announced, placing a hand on his chest and lowering it down below his waist. She reached the midpoint of his sweatpants and the grin that grew on his lips told her that she had said just the right words he needed to hear.

Thirty minutes, Athena had managed to knock her man out with her talented mouth. He was now fast asleep with his arm wrapped around her. Sleeping was what she intended to do, but her thoughts kept her up thinking about something else. Something that had been bugging her all day.

Athena gently eased out of his arms, crept out of bed and went to her walk-in closet on the other side of the bedroom. She switched on the lights to reveal her modern, yet feminine spaced closet. Then she went straight over to her Chanel bag that sat on a shelf above her clothing.

Once bringing it down, she opened it and brought out the pregnancy test box. Athena placed her bag back in its original spot and headed to the bathroom to take her test.

Thirty minutes later and she was staring down at two lines.

Positive.

"Fuck," she cursed.

She was pregnant and even though that's exactly what she and Keon had just discussed wanting, it was the last thing she wanted now. Especially because she wasn't sure if the child growing inside of her was even Keon's.

CHAPTER 16

1 MONTH LATER

"5 0's party should be lit."

"For the amount of people I'm letting that nigga bring up in my casino, it better be."

"Nah, it's definitely gonna be lit 'cause I'll finally be able to meet this mystery girl that's had you so sprung these days."

Kalmon looked up from the checkered board to stare into the eyes of Jahmai. He shot him an emotionless look before focusing back on the board and moving his black chess piece ahead, resulting in him capturing one of Jahmai's pieces, and taking it off the board.

"She's coming right?" Jahmai questioned his cousin, leaning forward in his seat to get a closer look at the chess board as he accessed his next move.

"She's welcome to if she wants to," Kalmon simply said, which made Jahmai look up to give him a confused expression.

"You have invited her though?"

Kalmon said nothing as he examined Jahmai making his next move.

"Really, nigga?" Jahmai let out a chuckle. "You really are tryna keep this girl a total secret."

"It wasn't my idea for us to be a secret in the first place," Kalmon announced, making another chess move and capturing Jahmai's piece again. "It was hers."

"Why?"

"She didn't want ladies at the Enterprise hating on her and I wasn't trying to make her feel uncomfortable so I agreed."

"Why would they be hating on... oh, I get it. Your secret admirers wouldn't approve of you breaking the marketing director's back."

Kalmon grinned without saying a word and kept playing their chess game.

"How long have you two been messing around?" Jahmai asked, frowning when he saw Kalmon's advantage over his chess pieces.

"Just under two months."

"And no one's clocked you two at the company yet?"

"Nope," Kalmon confirmed.

"Not even your mom?"

Kalmon shook his head no.

"We do a good job of acting like we can't stand each other, so no one's suspected a thing. Besides, I'm not in so often."

"And if they do suspect something, would that change things between you and her?"

Kalmon contemplated to himself privately for a while, thinking about whether or not his situation with Azia becoming public knowledge would change things between him and her.

"I wouldn't let it," he stated, coolly. "She didn't want anyone finding out at the company but if they do then it is what it is. I won't let her end things and she knows that. We might not be in a relationship, but she's been mine for the past month and she'll continue to be mine."

Kalmon then made his final chess move on the board before voicing, "Checkmate."

"Fuck," Jahmai cursed before sucking his teeth. "You caught me at a bad time. I woulda smoked your ass."

"Oh you mean like the last time you tried to smoke my ass and I beat you instead?"

"Man, shut up."

Kalmon laughed heartily at Jahmai's bitterness due to his defeat.

"But back to your girl though; well not your official girlfriend, but your girl. I still think you should invite her to the party."

"You only want me to invite her so your nosy ass can meet her."

"Yeah and what?" Jahmai cheekily smiled at his cousin. "I gotta see the girl that managed to have you so whipped after you swore you were staying away from commitment because of your ex."

"Technically, Azia and I are not in a relationship," Kalmon reminded him. "We're just kickin' it."

"Kickin' it?"

"Yup."

"Well if that's what you want to call it after you've seen every part of her body then cool, nigga. But you can't keep her a secret forever, especially if you're gonna keep seeing her and keep "kickin' it".

"I can't force her to come if she doesn't want to."

"You don't even know that 'cause you haven't invited her, Kal. Just invite he—"

The sound of the front door opening was heard and both Kalmon and Jahmai looked over at the corridor leading to the entrance, waiting to see who it was. Diamond raced from her bed to the front door. Kalmon already knew who it was and even though it was very unexpected, he was glad about who had come.

"Hey D! You okay baby girl? You been a good girl? Yes, yes you have been."

Kalmon could already hear her greeting Diamond and he grinned at the fact that they'd gotten even closer over the past few weeks. Jahmai had no idea who was coming over, but when he saw a breathtaking woman appear in the corridor and the way Kalmon raced out of his seat to greet her, he knew exactly who this was.

"Zi," he greeted her lovingly. "You didn't say you were coming over."

Azia watched as he came up to her and pulled her in for a hug. The second he was near, she could smell his seductive aroma and it sent her mind into pure bliss. And when he wrapped his large arms around her, Azia's insides melted. Then he lifted her chin and deeply kissed her for a few seconds.

"I left my favorite lip gloss behind last night and wanted to pick it up," she explained before her eyes drifted to the handsome figure observing her from his seat.

Noticing her attention shift, Kalmon knew it was time to do the introductions.

"Azia, this is my cousin Jahmai and Jahmai this is Azia."

Jahmai was no eyesore to the eyes. Those mahogany pools of his made him very easy on the eyes. His coffee brown skin was smooth as ever, with not a single scar or spot in sight. He had a bushy beard extending out from his jawline and a goatee below his bottom lip. Small locs sat on the top of his head that were currently neatly tied back away from his face and the sides of his head were cut into a low fade. He was a beautiful man, there was no doubt about it.

"About time I meet the girl that I've heard so much about," Jahmai announced with a grin, getting up from his seat. He was over the moon that Azia had just walked into Kalmon's condo, allowing him to meet her just as he'd wanted to.

"It's nice to meet you, Jahmai." Azia greeted him, watching him come closer to where she stood with Kalmon holding her. "Kalmon's mentioned you a couple times."

Once Jahmai was nearer, Kalmon let go of her and stepped out of the way.

"Good things mentioned I hope?"

"Of course," she promised, beaming up at him. Just like Kalmon, Jahmai was tall but Kalmon still had him by a couple inches.

"Good, that way I don't have to fuck his ass up."

Kalmon cocked his head slightly to the side as he locked eyes with his cousin, knowing fully well that Jahmai couldn't take him one-on-one. Maybe if he had help, but even then, Kalmon could still effortlessly beat him up and his helpers.

Jahmai brought out his hand to shake Azia's and she willingly took it, smiling wider as she did so. The only family of Kalmon's that she'd ever met was his mom who she worked for, so to be meeting a different family member had her gassed.

"So you came all this way for your lip gloss?" Jahmai queried with his left brow hiked up in the air. "Damn, you women don't play about your make up."

"It's my favorite gloss," she preached. "Fenty gloss and I honestly go crazy without it."

She does, Kalmon mused to himself as he watched the pair of them interact while wrapping an arm around Azia's waist, keeping her close to him.

"I see," Jahmai replied with a nod before adding, "I see you've also got a key."

Kalmon threw Jahmai a side eye but Jahmai chose to ignore it while keeping his attention on Azia.

"Oh yeah, Kal told me to pick up Diamond one time he was out of the city and babysit so he had the front desk give me a spare key. He made me keep it so I've had it ever since."

She's got a key already and she's taking care of Diamond? Yeah this nigga is in a relationship whether he knows it or not and is definitely falling for her. Hard.

"Makes sense," Jahmai stated, noticing the way they were linked close by Kalmon's arm. "Are you coming on Friday?"

"Coming to what?"

Kalmon felt his frustrations instantly mount at the fact that Jahmai had brought up the subject of Friday. Something he was hoping to discuss with Azia much later.

"50 cent's rented out Kalmon's casino for his private birthday party. He's having a casino themed event and wanted Kal's casino only. It's going to be a big night. You should come through."

"Ease up, Jah. She might have better things to do than to spend the night partying away with a bunch of strangers," Kalmon commented.

"Actually I don't," Azia chimed in. "I'd love to come. Thank you for the invite, Jahmai."

"It was my pleasure, love." Jahmai gave her a warm smile before looking over at Kalmon and still smiling.

A few minutes later, Jahmai said his goodbyes to his cousin and Azia before making his departure out of Kalmon's condo.

"Why didn't you invite me to 50's party? Don't you want me to come?"

Kalmon gazed into her hazel eyes, seeing the worry cradled with them. And he knew that it was his job to melt that worry away.

"I didn't invite you because I figured you wouldn't want to come."

"And how did you figure that one out?" she asked him with an arched brow.

"Well..." He paused briefly, lifting up her thighs and placing them onto his lap. "You were the one that wanted us to remain a secret, right?"

Azia watched as he palmed her right foot and began massaging it.

They were currently sitting on his sofa outside on his terrace, looking at the breathtaking city view with his outdoor fireplace lit.

"Yeah, but that doesn't mean we can't party together," she said with a light shrug. "I want to come, Kal. Only if you want me there."

"I definitely want you there Zi," he confirmed, lifting her feet to his lips and gently kissing it. Then he was back to rubbing on her feet and admiring her perfect white painted toenails.

"Okay." She smiled at the thought of partying with him. They'd never done that before.

"I can't wait to see you dressed up, looking sexier than you already do." Azia's cheeks turned red at his statement. "Invite Nova and Iman too, since they're back on speaking terms again."

She nodded in agreement. Thankfully, Kalmon's advice on getting them one-on-one and discussing the situation managed to work. Azia was then able to invite them both to her apartment and squash the beef. Things weren't completely back to normal because the girls wouldn't meet up unless Azia arranged it. And even when they met up, things still felt awkward. So they were back on speaking terms again but not back to their normal selves with each other. But Azia was hoping that the casino party did the trick to get Nova and Iman back to normal. Because if it didn't, she wasn't sure what she would do about them anymore.

* * *

"Athena, what's going on? You had me so worried on the phone."

Athena gave her sister a depressed look before sighing deeply. Then her eyes got misty and the first tear dropped out of her lids.

"Nana, no, no please don't cry," Iman pleaded with her sister, lifting her arm to her shoulder and pulling her in towards her. "Tell me what's wrong."

Athena allowed her sister to pull her close and comfort her with a hug. While Iman stroked her back, Athena's tears came out stronger and soaked into Iman's hoodie.

"Talk to me, please sis," Iman continued to beg.

Athena sobbed for a few more seconds before breaking away from Iman's embrace and wiping away her falling tears. Then she locked eyes with her older sister.

"I need you to come with me to my appointment."

"Your appointment?" Iman's suspicious expression formed. "What appointment?"

"My appointment with my doctor."

"Okay. Is everything okay?" Iman queried, feeling her heart race as she feared the worst. "Are you sick?"

"No," Athena voiced. "I'm not sick."

"So what's going on?"

"I'm having an abortion."

"WHAT?!"

Athena tore her eyes away from Iman to look outside the car window, observing her home that she had just come out of. Athan was still at school and Keon still at work, leaving her all alone.

"What do you mean you're having an abortion? Why?" Iman began pounding questions down Athena's way.

"I'm having an abortion because of Keon," she explained, making Iman shake her head with confusion.

"What? He told you to get one?"

"Yes," Athena confirmed. "He said he doesn't want another child right now and I don't want him unhappy, so I'm getting rid of it."

"What the fuck? This is your body though; you're the one carrying the child, not him. What the fuck is he talking abo—"

"Iman please!" Athena yelled, making Iman jump slightly in her seat. "I've already made my decision. I just don't want to go through it alone. That's why I need my big sister to support me."

"Are you sure you've thought this through properly, sis. You don't have to do thi—"

"Please Iman," Athena interrupted her, sending a look of desperation her way. "I need your support today. I can't do this alone. And if you truly love me as your sister, you'll do this for me."

Iman continued to stare at her sister with worry. Having an abortion wasn't something that Iman would have ever expected from her sister and to find out that Keon had been the one to put her up to this, made anger boil inside her. But at the end of the day, this was her younger sister and she promised to always be there for her no matter what.

"Okay. Let's go," Iman concluded, starting the engine of her car and heading to Athena's appointment.

CHAPTER 17

YOU CAN FIND ME IN THE CLUB, BOTTLE FULL OF BUB

> Look mami I got the X if you into taking drugs
> I'm into having sex, I ain't into making love
> So come give me a hug if you into to getting rubbed

Azia had never been to a casino before. Gambling wasn't really her forte at all. She'd always believed that the only time she would step into a casino would be when she finally visited Las Vegas. However tonight, she was in the hottest casino of the entire New York State. The entire casino was popping with people playing various games from poker, roulette, slot machines and more. There was also a dance floor and a bar area with sparking white lights. The man of the night, 50 Cent, was currently at one of the tables playing a game of roulette with his gorgeous date, Instagram model, Nikki Nicole, by his side.

Azia honestly couldn't believe her eyes. This entire establishment was a sight indeed. It had the theme colors of gold, bright red and bright yellow. Even the casino staff had attractive uniforms with the men wearing navy silk shirts and black bowties. Whereas the women wore navy silk dresses that stopped above their knees and black stilettos on their feet. To know that the man she had relations with owned this entire casino made her gassed. He really was a businessman, and a successful one at that.

"It's really lit tonight! Thank you for inviting me, Zi!"

Azia arrived less than ten minutes ago with her girls and they were now posted up at the bar, trying to get a few drinks for themselves.

"You know I got you, Va. I had to bring along my two favorite girls in the whole wide world," Azia replied to Nova before grabbing each of her best friends' hands. "I just need you guys to be good again. I'm tired of all this tension. I miss us."

Both Nova and Iman looked over at each other without saying anything. They both had neutral looks on their faces but Azia knew better. Neutral was the last thing on either of their minds.

"Come onnnnnnn," Azia pleaded. "I need my girls back."

Azia observed as her friends continued to stare each other down before Iman slowly cracked a smile and then Nova broke out into one too.

"I'm sorry again for... you know, for being so harsh about your relationship with Caesar. I never should have been so rude about your situation," Iman apologized, letting go of Azia's hand to slide in between Azia and Nova. "I'm sorry."

"And I'm sorry too, for calling you out about not having a man and throwing a drink on you. I never should have done that shit, Iman."

"Yeah you shouldn't have but you can really apologize by buying me drinks all night long. And a new handbag tomorrow morning."

"Deal," Nova agreed with a giggle.

Nova smiled happily and opened her arms to embrace Iman. The pair of them hugged and Azia's elation made her feel giddy inside. She started clapping before joining her best friends and hugging them lovingly.

The girls then focused back on the bar and drinking their drinks before heading to the main casino.

> I'll take you to the candy shop
> I'll let you lick the lollipop
> Go 'head girl don't you stop
> Keep going 'til you hit the spot, whoa

Despite the various casino games going on the casino floor, it seemed as if everyone's attention had shifted onto the three black beauties that had just stepped into the room. Everyone's eyes landed on them and each girl could feel her nerves bubbling up inside. Azia especially, who wasn't used to this many eyes on her unless she was in an important meeting.

"Can I escort you beautiful ladies to a table?"

The girls looked in the direction of the voice to see a pretty ebony skinned woman dressed in uniform.

"No, we're okay," Iman responded, deciding to take the lead on getting her girls through the room. "Thank you though."

The woman nodded, giving them a friendly smile before leaving and heading back into the room.

Iman linked arms with her girls and headed to the first table that she laid eyes on.

"So girls what do you think about us playing po…" Her words trailed off once she got closer to the table and laid eyes on the man currently playing a game of poker with an interested audience.

"Iman," Keon called out to her, pleased to see her. "I didn't know you were coming out tonight."

Iman said nothing to him and just continued to stare at him.

"Athena hates casinos but you don't by the look of things."

Looking into the eyes of the man that had made her sister get an abortion, resulted in every muscle inside her body to tense up.

"Let's go to another table," Iman told her best friends, turning away to look at a different table.

"What's wrong with this on—"

"It's not the right one for us. We're going," Iman ordered, pulling her girls over to the next table.

The next table that had the one man that had been racing through Azia's mind. When she saw him at the center table, playing a game of roulette her heart skipped a couple of beats. But when his eyes locked on hers, her stomach did somersaults.

Seeing the way Azia's eyes had connected to the handsome Howard brother at the table made Iman grin and lead her friends closer towards it.

"I've found the perfect table."

Once they were at the table, Azia, Nova and Iman each stood at the other side of the table watching Kalmon who sat the head of the table. There was also a small crowd watching Kalmon playing blackjack with a few other men, and by the looks of things, he was beating the dealer. The girls watched for several minutes, actually interested in the game, especially due to the man who was effortlessly winning.

"He's actually good at this," Nova commented while they continued to watch Kalmon play. "No wonder he owns the biggest casino in the city."

"And he's still winning, despite the fact that he can't stop looking at you," Iman stated, gently nudging Azia's arm.

It was true. All throughout Azia's time at the table with her girls watching Kalmon play, Kalmon didn't stop looking at Azia. And it wasn't just quick glances; he was giving her long stares and still hadn't lost his concentration in the game.

Azia's body got warmer with each passing second the more their stare down continued. He hadn't even said one word to her yet and here her body was, craving him, wanting to feel his touch.

Eventually the game ended and Kalmon had indeed won. And just when Azia came up with the suggestion of the girls moving on to the next table, Kalmon got up out of his seat and made his way over to where Azia stood.

The baby pink off the shoulder maxi dress that hugged her body like second skin was doing everything to him right now. Everything that was telling him to take her away from this place and have her all to himself.

"Well if it isn't the man responsible for this entire night," Iman piped up, carefully looking at Kalmon.

She hadn't seen him since Athan's last birthday but even with all the time that had passed, Kalmon still looked as attractive as ever.

"Iman," Kalmon warmly greeted her. "It's nice to see you again. It's been a minute."

"It has," Iman agreed. "Thanks for the invite."

"Yes, thank you for the invite," Nova chimed in. "It's good to meet the man behind this amazing night."

"Nova, right?" Nova confirmed his query with a nod. "It's nice to meet you too. You all look stunning tonight," he complimented the ladies.

"Thank you but we all know the woman who looks the most stunning to you is…" Iman's eyes drifted over to Azia who was now blushing bright red. "We'll give you two some privacy."

"Privacy? I wanted to see them toget—"

"Come on, Va. We can spy on them from a distance," Iman voiced, pulling Nova along, leaving Kalmon and Azia alone.

They hadn't said a word to one another yet, but there was no need, because their eyes and energy were doing more than enough talking. But for Kalmon, that wasn't enough.

He reached for her hand and gently led her through the casino to the dancefloor on the other side. When they arrived, Kalmon carefully stood behind her, placing his hands on the side of her waist. Azia followed his lead and began to grind her body on his, enjoying the moment that had started between them.

"You look breathtaking tonight, Zi." She smiled at his words. "I just want to take you away from here. Now."

Their bodies continued to dance in sync to the upbeat song.

"You don't look so bad yourself."

One thing that Azia loved about seeing Kalmon in suits was that he wasn't boring like everyone else in their typical black suits. She had already seen him in a navy suit and a gray one, but tonight he was wearing a purple tuxedo blazer with a matching purple silk bow tie, a black shirt, black pants and black lace-ups on his feet. All his jewelry was gold; a gold chain hanging around his neck and a flashy gold watch secured around his wrist. He looked too sexy tonight.

"I'm really glad you're here tonight."

"I'm really glad I made it out tonight too."

"And I really can't wait for this night to be over so that you and I..."

His sweet whispers trailed off and Azia turned to look at him, eager to hear more.

"So that you and I?" she piped up, encouraging him to finish his sentence.

"So that you and I..." He placed a kiss on her neck. "Can head home…" Another kiss. "Where I'll be able to get you…" Another kiss. "Out of this dress…" He kept pecking her skin. "Completely nake—"

"I can definitely see now why you've decided to give up on us."

The voice of the one woman he wasn't expecting at all or even trying to see was now the one echoing in his ears. He looked ahead and his face immediately scrunched up at the woman standing a short distance away from where he stood with Azia.

"What the fuck are you doing here?"

Just by his tone and how he suddenly became distant, with his hands no longer on her and him no longer standing behind her, told Azia that he was pissed. But those weren't the only things that gave him away. It was the anger radiating from his body.

"It's a party, Kalmon," she responded with a lopsided grin. "I came here to party, but you on the other hand"—she glanced at Azia and gave her a dirty look—"it looks like you had other plans in mind tonight, Kalmon." Her eyes focused back on Kalmon. "Is this the girl you've decided to choose over me? Well she's nothing compared to m—"

"If I have to drag your dumb ass outta here my damn self then best believe I'll do just that, Jahana," he snapped, stepping closer towards her. "I want you of here. Now."

"I'm not going anywhere!" she yelled. Her yell caused party members to look over at them. "You've tried to push me away for this long but I'm not letting you do it any longer, Kalmon! I'm not losing you to this hoe right he—"

"Call her out of her name again. I fuckin' dare you," Kalmon said in a tone that sent chills down Azia's spine. She wasn't the person on the receiving end of his threat, but here she was, feeling the aftermath.

"You're trying to cause a scene and that shit is only going to backfire on you, Jahana. You keep playing with your life like that shit is funny. Is death funny to you?"

Azia had never heard Kalmon speak like this before to someone else. Sure, she had heard him say some of the craziest things, but she never heard him threaten a person's life before with no remorse. Especially not a woman that happened to be his ex.

"Now I'm only going to tell you this one time and one time only," he instructed tensely. "Get your ass out of here and go home. If I see that you're still here then that will be your confirmation to me that you indeed want to play with your life. You got the right nigga to put you in the wrong mothafuckin' place tonight. So play all you want to."

After his announcement, Kalmon walked back over to Azia and stood behind her, placing his hands back on her body and moving his body in time with the music, encouraging her to do the exact same. Jahana backed away from the pair with a scowl on her face.

"You're going to regret this, Kalmon," she muttered under her breath as she left the dancefloor.

He was acting as if nothing had happened and Azia didn't like it. It was as if his ex-girlfriend hadn't just popped up out of nowhere and interrupted their moment together.

"Kalmon, you can't be seriously trying to act like that didn't happen?" Azia questioned him, frowning as their bodies moved together perfectly.

"Fix your face, baby girl," he ordered. "I can't have you unhappy over some shit that doesn't matter."

"How doesn't she matter when she's clearly still in love with yo—"

"Boss."

Azia turned around to see who she had been interrupted by and it was a man dressed in an all-black suit.

"There's a situation on the main floor with your manager and two ladies that accompanied your woman. Security was ready to take them out, but your brother and cousin intervened, telling us to fall back."

His woman.

Azia couldn't help but love the way that sounded, but at the same time, she still had her apprehensions about him because of the situation that had just gone down with Jahana. However, loving the sound of things and thinking about her doubts wasn't important right now.

"Nova and Iman you mean?" Azia asked the fair skinned man. "What's going on?"

Kalmon, Azia and the suited man who Azia figured was one of his employees, headed back to the main casino room only for her mouth to drop open when she saw Nova shouting hysterically.

"Let me the fuck go! I need to beat his ass for lying to me!"

"Caesar, who is this woman?" The light skinned woman standing next to Caesar with a baby bump asked.

"I'm the woman he's been sleeping with behind your back!" Nova shouted.

"What? Caesar, is this true?"

"Yes it's true!" Nova answered on Caesar's behalf to his wife. "It's all fucking true! He's nothing but a liar and a cheat!"

From the looks of things, Kalmon's cousin, Jahmai was currently the one holding Nova back. Whereas Iman was taking off her earrings and had kicked off her heels, but Keon was not letting her get past him.

Azia rushed over to where they all were and a small crowd formed around them in the main casino area.

"Nova! Iman! What the hell is going on?"

"The stupid nigga is married! With a whole wife!" Nova bellowed, trying her chance at getting closer to Caesar but failed instantly due to the man keeping her at bay. This man that she didn't even know. "A pregnant wife!"

"And I'm more than ready to beat his ass for lying to my best friend!" Iman shouted. "Get the hell out of my way, Keon. Now!"

"Now you know I can't do that, Iman. You need to calm down."

"Don't tell me to calm down!" Iman fired back at him, her chest heaving up and down. "Just move!"

"Your husband is a lying, cheating asshole." Nova spoke directly to Caesar's wife, who was shocked by the entire ambush and revelation. "He gave me this ring and made me believe that one day he would marry me when really he's been married this whole time!"

"Nova, I'm sorry," Caesar spoke up apologetically.

"You're sorry?" She let out a loud laugh. "YOU'RE SORRY?"

Seeing that Nova was trying to make a move again on Caesar made Jahmai continue to keep her away, holding her tight with his arms around her waist. Keeping her as near to him as possible.

"Why the fuck won't you let me go?" Nova mean mugged him, feeling her frustrations mount the more she realized she wasn't any closer to hurting Caesar.

It would never compare to the hurt she felt but it was worth a shot. She needed him to feel pain as punishment for what he had done to her.

"Because what you're tryna do ain't worth it, shorty," Jahmai said in a tone only loud enough for her to hear. "He ain't worth it. A beauty like you should never embarrass yourself like this for no man."

After saying those final words, Jahmai finally released her from his hold.

There was a mixture of things that Nova felt but right now the number one thing was heartbreak. Heartbreak out of this world. It felt like every part of her body had been sliced open to form fresh wounds. Wounds that she didn't think could ever be soothed and sealed again.

Instead of doing what she so badly wanted to do, she decided to take what little dignity she had left and leave the casino. Azia raced after her and just when Iman was about to do the same, she realized Keon was still blocking her way. She put her heels back on before pushing past him and rushing to her friend's rescue. Because after this horror of a night, Nova needed all the rescuing she could get.

CHAPTER 18

4 *am.*

After getting to Nova, Iman and Azia stayed by her side for the rest of the night and remained her shoulders to cry on once they were driven in an Uber to Nova's home. They hadn't left her side until seeing that she was fast asleep in her bed.

"That idiot has ruined her life. I didn't want to be right but he really wasn't the one for her. I hoped to God that I had been wrong and just talking my usual Iman shit but fuck, Azia. She really loved him."

Iman's words repeated in her head as she placed her key in her door and entered her apartment. After the night that she had just had, all Azia wanted to do was climb in her bed and sleep this entire night away. She was hoping deep down that she could sleep away this nightmare and hopefully when she woke up this night would disappear like it never happened.

Ding!

Azia opened up her YSL side bag, bringing out her phone to see a new text message from Kalmon.

You home?

She sent him the thumbs up emoji and locked her phone, dropping it on the edge of her bed followed by her bag.

Ding!

She sighed once another text notification sounded off.

Yes or no?

Kalmon.

Azia: *Yes, I'm home.*

Kalmon: *Yeah, I know.*

Kalmon: *Come open the door.*

Azia: *I'm trying to sleep right now Kalmon.*

Kalmon: *No you ain't.*

Kalmon: *The door.*

Azia: *I am.*

Kalmon: *How you trying to sleep when you just entered your apartment less than five minutes ago?*

Kalmon: *And you're fully dressed still.*

Azia: *How do you know that?*

Kalmon: *You don't need to worry about that.*

Kalmon: *Just come and open the door.*

Kalmon: *I won't tell you again.*

Even though she was reluctant to let him into her home, she did it anyway. And when she told him she wanted to go change out of her dress and would be with him shortly, he gripped her arm, keeping her in her stance.

"Kalmon, I need to—"

The second her head looked up at him, he branded his lips down to hers and kissed her with an urgency that ignited her soul. He was able to do the one thing he'd wanted to all night but never had the opportunity to do until now. And when his lips pulled away from hers, her eyes fluttered open and she deeply gazed at him.

"I apologize about Jahana," he announced, lifting a hand to her cheek and caressing it. "She never should have been at the casino tonight."

"But I'm actually kinda glad that she was," Azia responded, removing his hand off her face and stepping back. "Cause it's reminded me of how she's still in love with you."

"That ain't got shit to do with me or you, Zi," he voiced, inching back towards her. "She means nothing to me."

"Oh believe me, I know." Azia gave him a sure look. "You threatened to kill her if she didn't obey you."

Kalmon gave her a blank stare.

"Is that something you do often? Threatening the lives of others?"

"Only when necessary," he explained, coolly. "Is that a problem?"

"What kinda question is that?" Azia asked incredulously. "Of course it's a problem, Kalmon. How can you willingly just threaten the lives of others?"

"When they threaten my wellbeing or the wellbeing of the people I love, I'll threaten whoever, whenever."

Azia gave him one last gaze before heading to her bedroom, purposely making sure she took the route away from Kalmon, not wanting to be stopped by him again. Only this time, instead of being stopped by him, he followed her into her bedroom.

"Azia, I don't want you mad at me. Just tell me what I can do to fix what's wrong," he said, watching her slide her off dress and walk over to her wardrobe to get her robe. "Nothing's wrong."

"You know better than to lie to me."

Once her silk robe was on, she headed to her bathroom and Kalmon was fast on her trail.

"Your ex is still in love with you, Kalmon."

"And what exactly do you want me to do about that? I can't force her to stop loving me."

He leaned against her doorframe, watching her stand in front of her mirror and take her make up off. She opened up her cupboard under her sink to bring out her tools that she needed.

"I'm not saying that you should do that. It's just got me thinking that messing around with you just might not be a good idea anymore."

Kalmon's face contorted with anger.

"What?"

Azia said nothing while continuing to wipe off her make up with her cotton pads and micellar water.

"You tryna end things between us? That's what you're tryna do?"

"I never said I was ending things," she fired back. "I said I was think—"

"What you said was bullshit," he retorted. "You know why I ended things with Jahana months ago. I told you that shit already but clearly you've gotten amnesia and forgotten so let me remind your ass. She disrespected my mom and it made me realize I have no real feelings for her. Her still being in love with me is her own personal problem."

Azia stepped on her silver step trashcan, throwing her cotton pads away before washing her face thoroughly with her facial wash. While she washed, Kalmon continued to talk.

"You're really about to let my ex come between us when I told you that she's nothing to me. You're the one who means something to me, Azia. How many times do you want me to reiterate this shit?"

Azia rinsed her face for a few more moments before reaching for her face towel hanging by the sink and drying her face. Once it was dry, she hung her towel back up before turning her body completely to face Kalmon who was no longer leaning against the doorframe. Instead, he now stood tall and bold in the center of her doorway with his arms crossed against his chest.

"I think we need a break."

"We don't need shit."

"I think we do, Kalmon," she pushed. "What are we even doing?"

"You know what we're doing Azia," he stated, entering her bathroom. "Don't act crazy. You know what this is."

"Kalmon, I can't—"

"You can't what?"

Now there was a small gap between them. A gap that Kalmon was anxious to close, but the words that she uttered made him stay put.

"I can't fall in love with you."

He looked at her like she had just shot a bullet through his heart.

"But that's exactly what's happening," she added. "And I'm scared. I'm scared you're going to break my heart; the same way you broke Jahana's heart."

Kalmon stepped forward and closed the gap between them.

"I'm not going to break your heart Zi."

"But how you can be so sure of that?"

"Because I just want what's best for you," he promised. "It's me though, I'm what's best for you."

Azia felt his hands hold her face and tilt her head up so that the only place she was looking was into those heavenly eyes of his.

"I don't trust anyone in life except my family and now you, Azia. You're the woman I trust and the only woman I want. Don't doubt that shit, Zi. I told you before that I've got you and I stand by that shit 100%. I won't break your heart."

He kissed her forehead and slowly started wrapping his arms around her, allowing Azia to happily drown in his cologne. She settled deeper into his body and wrapped her arms around too.

"I don't want you worrying about Jahana. She's not going to be a problem. And I don't want you scared about us when you know how good we are together. A'ight?"

Azia looked up at him and nodded, believing him. Then they sealed lips and kissed like two lovers dependent to live by their lips staying joined together. At this point, Azia was hopeful for the future between her and Kalmon. She was also becoming less doubtful about Jahana being a problem for them. But the doubts were still there. She just hoped that her doubts didn't prove to be right.

CHAPTER 19

Nova I'm so sorry baby. Just let me explain. You can't ignore me forever. I love you and I'm not letting you go.

Send.

He had sent her over a dozen messages and called her all weekend, but still she hadn't bothered answering any or responding. She was pissed with him and that was the last thing he wanted her to be because he actually loved Nova. Despite the fact that he had done her dirty, she still meant a lot to him. He hadn't even known that she would come out to 50's party because she hadn't mentioned it to him. Now that he thought about it, he had never brought it up in their conversations because he never discussed work with her.

Ding!

Caesar immediately checked his phone, his heart skipping a beat at the thought of seeing Nova's name appear on his screen. However, it wasn't her.

You fucked up last week. Hopefully this doesn't mess things up for us.

Unknown.

It won't. It was just a little mishap, he typed back.

Unknown: *Remember we have a job to do. Stop fucking around and get your ass in line.*

Caesar: *I got it all under control.*

Caesar: *We're going to take what's ours.*

* * *

Today was Monday, which meant that three days had passed since 50 Cent's casino party. Keon purposely waited the weekend out so that he could do the one thing he was about to do right now. He opened the front door of her shop, making the door's bell chime as he stepped through.

It was 12:30pm and even though the bakery opened 30 minutes ago, it was still occupied with customers. Various people sat at the oak round tables, drinking or either eating a sweet snack. There was also a short queue of people at the checkout section, waiting to be served.

His eyes darted around the bakery's modern interior and when he couldn't see who he was looking for, he decided to head through to the door at the back of the shop, labelled staff only.

It didn't take long for him to get to her office door and without bothering to knock, he turned the knob only to frown when he realized it was locked.

"What the? Iman!"

Knock! Knock!

"Open the door," he demanded, knocking louder on the oak door. "You can't ignore me no—"

"Don't flatter yourself," her soft voice sounded from behind him, making him turn to see her standing with her bag and MacBook in hand. "You're not that important."

She brought out her key from her bag and when he saw that she was about to open her door, he stepped away to give her some space. Seeing that she had just arrived to work made him feel slightly more at ease because thinking that she had locked herself away from him made his heartache.

"Look Iman," he began, as he observed her keying her door and pushing it open. "I came to check up on you after what happened on Friday night with your girl and wanted to make sure that we were cool."

She strode into her office and he was fast on her heels, closing her door behind him.

"We're not," she retorted, dropping her items onto her desk then twisting around to face him. "You should leave."

He didn't understand where this attitude had suddenly come from. He and Iman had always been cool. They'd never had any problems and she was always friendly to him. But at the night of the casino party, she treated him like he was nothing to her. And that infuriated him more than anything.

"Iman, what's gotten into you?" he asked her, firmly. "You treat me like shit at the party and now you treat me like shit today. What the hell have I done to you?"

"Nothing. Just leave me alone."

Iman then went around her desk and took her seat on her velvet pink chair.

"I'm not going anywhere until you talk to me."

She saw him come close to her desk and stare down at her in a way that made her breathing become shallower. Even though she was sure of her newfound hatred for him, he still had an effect on her and she hated it.

"We have nothing to talk about, Keon, so you should just get the hell out of my office. If you came to get cupcakes for my sister who you claim to love, then go to the main checkout and someone will happily serve you."

"I told you I don't want no one else serving me but yo—"

"I'm sure as hell never serving you ever again and don't want anything to do with you, so get out."

Keon's eyes refused to break from hers and his lips remained straight. Clearly, he had done something wrong to Iman but the million-dollar question was what?

"Your sister that I claim to love?" He repeated her words, letting them circulate in his thoughts. "What's that supposed to mean?"

"Exactly what it means," Iman bitterly stated, cutting her eyes at him. "Just leave, Keo—"

"Nah fuck all this," he fumed, suddenly circling her desk and making his way around to her.

He had come over so quickly that Iman didn't even have time to register what the hell was happening. But by the time he had come over, she was out of her seat and leaning against her desk with him standing right in front of her; all because he had gotten her out her seat.

"I'm tired of you talking to me like I'm some bitch ass nigga," he snapped. "Now either you tell me what the fuck is up or you get your ass fucked up. The choice is yours, Iman."

"You ain't gonna do shit," she replied with an eye roll. "Just get away from me."

She tried to push him away by his chest, but it was a failed attempt because that solid physique of his stayed right in place, right in front of her.

"Get away from me, Ke..." Her words paused once she realized where his hand currently was. Wrapped around her throat in a grip not too tight but not too loose either. It was a perfect hold and strangely, she liked it.

"Tell me what I've done," he ordered. "That's not a request either."

"You know what you've done."

Iman didn't understand why he was acting so oblivious to a situation that he caused.

"You know what you made my sister do."

Keon slowly let go of her neck, releasing her and sighing softly.

"She told you?"

"Of course she told me, I'm her sister!" Iman shouted at him, hitting his chest.

"Yo, chill Iman," he warned her. "It's not that deep."

"Not that deep?" Iman hit his chest again. "How could you put her through that shit? And make her go through it alone! You idiot!"

She tried to hit him again but this time he caught her wrists, stopping her from carrying out her plans.

"Make her go through it alone? I didn't make her go through shit alone. I'm always there for he—"

"No you weren't there for her! I was the one there for her. I was the only one there for her when she aborted your baby for you!"

Keon's heart stopped when he heard Iman's last yell and he instantly let go of her wrists.

"What?"

"You heard me!" Iman continued to shout. "You made her get an abortion and that's exactly what she did. I had to be the one to support her through it, not you."

Keon stepped back away from her and felt his eyes instantly get watery. Iman observed the way his fists were now clenched, the way his eyes were widening and the way his jaw was twitching. The deadly look in his eyes not only frightened her, but scared every bone in her body.

"She was pregnant?" he asked with disbelief and Iman's face began to soften once she realized how distraught he was by her revelation.

"Wait? You didn't know?"

"No," he snapped. "I thought you were talking about the doctor I made her go see with me. To help her get—" The past four weeks started rushing through his mind. How Athena had agreed to get pregnant again just before they walked down the aisle. She even suggested it. He talked to Athena about seeing a fertility doctor to assist them and despite her reluctance, she agreed to see the doctor and they were scheduled for an appointment tomorrow morning.

"Fuck!" Keon cursed, turning away from Athena.

How could the woman that he invested everything into betray him like this? She had aborted his child. Their child. And didn't even have the decency to tell him.

"I'm going to kill her," he said in a whisper, more so to himself than Iman, but she heard him loud and clear.

"No you're not, Key."

Iman moved off her desk to stand behind him. "Are you sure you didn't know?" she carefully asked. "She said she aborted it because you told her to."

"How the fuck could I say such a thing when we were trying to expand our family?" He turned back around to face her, towering over her. "Huh? How could I ever make her have a fuckin' abortion when I'm trying to build my family?"

"I'm sorry, Keon. She just made it seem like you were responsible."

"No, she's responsible! And I'm going to kill her," he concluded, ready to take his leave until Iman grabbed his arm and stopped him from leaving.

"Please, Keon. You need to calm down."

She could see how hurt he was and she knew that the hurt was making him say some crazy things right now. Killing Athena was something he could never do.

"Calm down?" He let out a hollow, callous laugh. "That's the last thing I'm about to do."

"I'm not letting you go," Iman announced boldly, gripping onto his arm tighter. He had on a short-sleeved Kenzo t-shirt, revealing his muscular arms. His muscular arm that Iman was currently holding onto that made her feel like she was holding onto a pure man. A pure man that had done nothing but love her sister, but she betrayed him.

"I can't let you do something stupid, Key. Not right now. I just need you to calm down. I know you're angry but maybe Athena has an explanation for why she did it."

"Fuck her explanation!" he exclaimed. "Her explanation means nothing to me after she's killed my kid! And for that I want her dead."

"Key, please, you don't mean that," Iman said to him in a begging tone. "You don't mean that because you're just angry and you have every right to be. What Athena has done is wrong and I'm sorry for even supporting her on it. I knew it was wrong but she really wanted my support so I gave it to her. I never should hav—"

Iman's words came to an instant halt because of his lips pressing up against hers, stopping her from speaking. It was a kiss that set off sparks around them and as cliché as that sounded, it was the truth. Their kiss was a powerful connection and something that Iman had imagined doing many times, but never in a million years thought would happen.

"Keon, no."

She immediately broke their kiss, pressing her hand against his chest to keep him at bay. She shyly gazed up at him, and seeing the way he was looking at her made her shyness worse.

"You're angry and you're just trying to get back at Athena," Iman informed him with a head shake. "This isn't right."

"Yes, I'm angry," he admitted, placing his hands to her waist. "Angry as fuck and still want to get out of here to strangle the fuck outta her, but this right here..." He leaned closer to her. "This right here feels righ—"

> When I die, put my money in the grave
> I really gotta put a couple niggas in they place
> Really just lapped every nigga in the race
> I really might tat "Realest Nigga" on my face

Both Iman and Keon looked down in the direction of where his phone was ringing. Iman ended up looking right in the middle of his pants, seeing the tent that had formed. Keon reached into his back pocket, his brows furrowing when he saw the unknown caller ID. It was an unknown caller but he already knew who it was.

"Stop fuckin' calling me, Jahana. I don't have time for your bullshit. You keep fuckin' with me like I won't put a bullet in your ass myself. Now do what the fuck I say."

Then he ended the call, turned off his phone and looked back over at Iman who was staring at him like he had grown two heads.

"Jahana?" she asked him. "Why's Kalmon's ex calling you?"

"Cause she's fuckin' crazy and won't listen," he explained with a shrug. "But she will. Forget about her though, like I was saying before, this right here feels right Iman."

"You're only saying that because Athena hurt you. You know it's not true," she told him, knowingly.

"It is true," he affirmed. "Because you're the one I wanted first, but she showed me more interest."

Iman said nothing, but her mind thought back to the time they first met at a mutual friend's party and how they had spoken first before Athena came along.

"That still doesn't change anything, Keon. You're with my sist—"

"No, I'm with you right now, Iman." He interrupted her before softly pecking her lips.

He kept on pecking her lips a few more times before their heated kiss commenced and Iman found herself kissing him back. Kissing him back like he was her man when he really belonged to her sister. But her sister had betrayed him. Betrayed him in the worst way.

"I want you Iman," he whispered in between his kisses that had now moved to her neck. "I know you want me too."

He was right. She'd wanted this man from the second she'd laid eyes on him, three years ago.

"And I'm about to give us what we both want by fucking you right now, right here."

Keon took off his white t-shirt, and pulled down his jeans and boxers. Taking off his shirt meant that his chest was on display and the sight of his tatted upper chest that Iman had never seen before made her attraction for this beautiful man build. Pulling down his boxers meant that Iman was able to catch sight of the largeness hanging between his thighs. Something that she'd dreamed about having but never envisioned actually having in real life.

Iman sensually moaned as his kisses continued along her neck, driving her crazy and before she knew it, she was allowing him to undress her. Allowing him to touch her in places that she'd never thought he would and allowing him to slide himself inside her, connecting them as one soul.

"Key... shit, that feels... that feels..."

"That feels what?" he questioned her, releasing her nipple from his mouth as he pushed deeper within her, smiling as her eyes rolled all the way back.

"Too fucking good, ahhhh," she whimpered as he thrusted back and forth.

The only problem was, two minutes into their session, Iman's phone wouldn't stop vibrating deep inside her bag but she was too caught up in the moment of having Keon's thickness and length inside her to even notice it. Neither of them noticed it. She was too caught up in the moment to realize that Athena was calling her, trying to tell her that she was seconds away from pulling up to her bakery with Athan who had a half day at pre-school so she thought it would be perfect to treat him to some fresh cupcakes from his auntie's bakery.

"You excited to see your aunt, baby boy?"

"Yes!"

"Good," Athena replied, parking her car in the bakery parking lot. "She'll be in her office so we'll head straight there to say hey before you get your cakes. Let's go, my love."

CHAPTER 20

Spending the entire weekend with Azia Price had been the only thing keeping him happy. Now he was forced to deal with the music of all the chaos that had gone down with his manager, Caesar. The Shade Room gossip blog managed to get various videos of the entire showdown between Caesar, his wife and Nova, and it wasn't looking good. This was bad press for the casino and that was one thing Kalmon couldn't allow.

Before heading to the casino to do damage control, Kalmon needed to pay Jahana a visit. The fact that she had caused a scene for him last Friday and called Azia out of her name meant that she was a problem. A problem he could no longer afford.

He was on his way to Jahana's apartment while on the phone with his father.

"Don't worry Dad, I've got it all under control. The casino will be just fine," Kalmon assured his father.

"I trust you'll handle this." His father's voice came through the car speakers. "And I trust that you and your brother are good?"

"Of course we're good," Kalmon replied with a frown. "Why wouldn't we be?"

"Last month, he told me that you have been making decisions without consulting him. Did he talk to you about it?"

"Yeah he did, but I already told him that I was simply making decisions that were going to benefit the both of us; our empire. But anyway, I did apolog—"

"You should be making decisions with your brother, Kal," his father interrupted him.

"And I have been," Kalmon confirmed, taking a left on the next road. "Like I was saying I did apologize for making decisions without him and I admit it was wrong. That's why Keon and I are expanding the legal aspect of things. Vaping is what's hot right now and we've decided to start a new company focused on that."

"That's really great to hear son. I'm glad things are better between you. You're not only brothers but you're a team. A team that trusts one another and works together."

"Keon and I trust each other, Dad. Why wouldn't we? We love each other and brothers stick together."

Minutes later, Kalmon pulled up to Jahana's apartment complex, and said his goodbyes to his dad before ending their call. Now it was time for Kalmon to deal with the woman that tried to drive a wedge between him and Azia. One thing he wasn't going to allow was his ex-girlfriend to destroy the new thing he was building with the woman he was falling for more and more each day.

"I want you out of my city, Jahana," he announced tensely, staring where she sat comfortably on her couch. "Tonight."

She let him into her home, actually glad to see him until she saw the white envelope in his hand. When he gave it to her and she opened it to see the plane ticket to her hometown, Atlanta, including a check for a half million dollars, her body began to heat up.

"I'm not going anywhere!" she yelled, chucking the ticket and check to the floor.

"Don't get found slumped over somewhere tryna fuck with me, Jahana," he threatened her with a stoic expression. "You're leaving tonight."

"How can you do this to me? After all the love I showed you, Kalmon. You and I were good together."

"After all the headaches you gave me, you mean?" He rose a brow at her. "Jahana, wake the fuck up! What we had is dead and was nothing more than sex. You know that."

"I hate you," she spat, getting up from her seat. "You ain't nothing but a bitch and the new bitch you're fuckin' with ain't nothing special either!"

Kalmon's eyes fixed on hers and the glare he gave her was enough to put the fear of death into her, but she chose to ignore it trying to act brave.

"I'll leave your city, Kalmon, but just know that everything you deserve is going to hit you like a ton of bricks. You think that you can get your way with every little thing."

The more she spoke, the more irritation coursed through his veins. He had only come to give her what she needed to get out of his city and he would be on his merry way out. Now was his cue to leave, so he started walking over to her door and was about to turn her knob until Jahana said something that made him freeze.

"You're going to pay for what you've done."

Her words had him confused and just as he turned around to face her, he saw the gun she was holding in her right hand. The gun didn't faze him; what fazed him is what she said.

"And what exactly have I don—"

Bang!

The gun went off and the bullet shot straight into his flesh, sending him straight to the floor.

"Ending us," she said. "That's what you're paying for, Kalmon."

Bang!

Then the next bullet came, entering him from the side. He tried to scream out but when he opened his mouth all that emerged was blood. If someone had told him months ago that this is how his life would end, he would have told them that they were nothing but a liar.

His vision was becoming blurry and he could feel his heart rate slowing down. His body was beginning to viciously shake and his entire body felt like it was on fire. He tried to lift his head up, but the intense pain radiating all over his body meant he failed. He couldn't bring himself to do anything but remain where he was, defenseless on the floor and now dying. Then the next words he heard from her made him question everything about the one man he thought he could trust in this life.

"I know you're sick of me calling you but I'm leaving you this voice-mail to let you know I've killed your brother Keon. Are you happy now? This is what you wanted, right?"

Then the darkness successfully pulled him in and he was out like a light.

To Be Continued…

A NOTE FROM MISS JEN

And we're back with another one! I hope you guys enjoyed this story and I can't wait for you to read the next one. Kalmon and Azia's story has only just begun and I hope you're ready for what's in store.

Please head over to my official website where you'll be able to see the visuals of Kalmon and Azia including the rest of the gang: www. missjenesequa.com. My website also includes **ALL** the visuals from my previous works, so don't hesitate to go check it out! And make sure you join my private readers group on Facebook to stay in touch with me and my upcoming releases: www.facebook.com/ groups/missjensreaders.
I'll be posting sneak peeks from the next book in my readers group, so make sure you're a part of it!

Thank you so much for reading! You readers mean the world to me and I'm never going to stop letting you guys know that.

Love From,
Jen xo

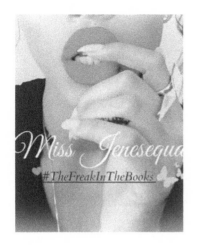

Miss Jenesequa is a best-selling African American Romance & Urban Fiction novelist. Her best-known works are 'Bad For My Thug', which debuted at #1 on the Amazon Women's Fiction Bestseller list, 'Loving My Miami Boss', 'He's A Savage But He Loves Me Like No Other' and 'Sex Ain't Better Than Love' which have all debuted top 5 on Amazon Bestseller lists.

Born and raised in London, UK where she always dreamed of becoming successful at anything she put her mind to. In 2013, she began writing full length novels and decided to publish some of her work online through Wattpad. The more she continued to notice how much people were enjoying her work, the more she continued to deliver. Royalty via Wattpad found Jenesequa and brought her on as a published author in 2015. Her novels are known for their powerful, convincing storylines and of course filled with drama, sex and passion. And they are definitely not for the faint-hearted. If you're eager and excited to read stories that are unique to any you've read before, then she's your woman.

Stay Connected

Miss Jenesequa's Reading Room

Feel free to connect personally with Miss Jenesequa at:
www.missjenesequa.com

Thank you so much for reading! Don't forget to leave a review on Amazon. I'd love to know what you thought about my novel. ♥

facebook.com/missjensworld
instagram.com/missjenesequa_

ALSO BY MISS JENESEQUA

Sex Ain't Better Than Love 1 & 2

Down For My Baller 1 & 2

Bad For My Thug 1 & 2 & 3

Addicted To My Thug 1 & 2 & 3

The Thug & The Kingpin's Daughter 1 & 2

Loving My Miami Boss 1 & 2 & 3

Crazy Over You: The Love Of A Carter Boss 1 & 2

Giving All My Love To A Brooklyn Street King 1 & 2

He's A Savage But He Loves Me Like No Other 1 & 2 & 3

Bad For My Gangsta: A Complete Novel

The Purest Love for The Coldest Thug 1 & 2 & 3

The Purest Love for The Coldest Thug: A Williams Christmas Novella

My Hood King Gave Me A Love Like No Other 1 & 2 & 3

My Bad Boy Gave Me A Love Like No Other: A Dallas Love Novella

The Thug That Secured Her Heart

Royalty Publishing House is now accepting manuscripts from aspiring or experienced urban romance authors!

WHAT MAY PLACE YOU ABOVE THE REST:

Heroes who are the ultimate book bae: strong-willed, maybe a little rough around the edges but willing to risk it all for the woman he loves.

Heroines who are the ultimate match: the girl next door type, not perfect - has her faults but is still a decent person. One who is willing to risk it all for the man she loves.

The rest is up to you! Just be creative, think out of the box, keep it sexy and intriguing!

If you'd like to join the Royal family, send us the first 15K words (60 pages) of your completed manuscript to submissions@royaltypublishinghouse.com

LIKE OUR PAGE!

Be sure to <u>LIKE</u> our Royalty Publishing House page on Facebook!